HORROR STORIES

JAMES FLYNN

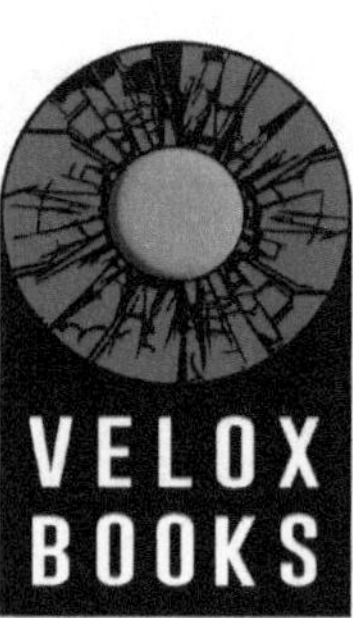

CONTENTS

BE CAREFUL WHAT YOU WISH FOR

There was a budding author
So young and smart and keen
He wrote a book of fiction
For everyone to read
But when the book was published
The readers didn't come
Faced with cold obscurity
It made him rather glum
But still the man persisted
He had a master plan
The world would see his story
Or else he would go mad

Truman sat in the dim light of his living room, staring at his computer screen with a morose expression. Up until this point, life had been going pretty well for him. He'd graduated from school, got a job at the local packing factory, and, perhaps most importantly, he'd finally moved out of his parents' house and moved into a studio apartment of his own. But despite all of this, there was still one hurdle, one life goal, that he was struggling to accomplish.

Truman was an aspiring author with a passion for books. Over the course of the last four years or so, he'd written a full-length novel, his debut masterpiece, and now he was faced with the daunting task of trying to get people to read it. Like every other self-published author, he'd put a ridiculous amount of time and effort into his book, followed by an even more ridiculous amount of time trying to promote the bloody thing. Every day he updated his social media accounts, he wrote blog posts, he made videos, he paid for online ads, and he even constructed clever little promotional deals wherever he could. You name it, he'd done it. And on days when he was feeling particularly brave and ambitious, he would even head out to his local high street and hand out cards and flyers for his book to pedestrians who made no effort whatsoever to look interested or curious. And of course, it was all proving itself to be a colossal waste of time.

Just writing the actual story had been a hard enough task for him. Countless evenings and sleepless nights had gone into crafting and refining the complex plot, as well as polishing the well-crafted characters. The story he'd created was great, and he knew it. It'd never be a commercial bestseller, what with the weird horror elements woven into it, but it wasn't Truman's goal to become a commercial bestselling author, anyway. His dream was to become a cult author, an underground cult author who had a small but extremely loyal following.

And with a book like his, he deserved it. Its title was *The Lottery Killer*, and it told the story of a deranged killer who was completely obsessed with the random chance of existence. The human race evolved by chance, and so every human being could be seen as the result of a natural lottery, or so the killer theorised. Homo sapiens evolved due to a series of chance environmental factors occurring over vast amounts of time, an individual baby was born due to the chance of its parents' timing, and therefore life itself was akin to a roll of a dice or the draw of a lottery ball. And if life was a lottery, thought the killer, death should also be one.

This was the killer's mission.

Throughout the various chapters of the book, the killer chooses his victims using a vintage lottery ball machine, the kind that has a wire frame that you turn with a handle, with each ball representing a random person's address. Then, once a ball is chosen, he visits the address and murders the resident in a horrific way. A signature is always left at the scene of the crime, the Lottery Killer's hallmark, where the eyes of the victim are gouged out and replaced with...yes, you guessed it: lottery balls. Then, as a symbolic finishing touch, a clock is placed in one of the dead person's hands to represent evolutionary time.

And the games didn't end there. The Lottery Killer always assembled an elaborate set of clues and puzzles around the nearest town, leading unsuspecting people to the location of his "works of art." This final part of his modus operandi also symbolised chance, in a way, for it depended on the luck or chance of random people finding the clues.

Truman's story was decent, and he was proud of what he'd created. It was edited well, it had a good front cover, and the marketing was being done, so by all means it should have been selling. But, for some unknown reason, it wasn't.

What he needed was some kind of outrageous or conspiratorial exposure for the book. He knew that most cult masterpieces had some kind of scandal or crime linked to them, a shocking real-life event that forges the title into the minds of the public, and this was exactly what his book was lacking.

The Catcher in the Rye had two assassinations linked to it, *A Clockwork Orange* inspired copycat groups of thugs to take to the streets of England, *American Psycho* had violent crimes linked to its grizzly pages, and *Fight Club* inspired groups of disgruntled youths to run amuck and cause criminal damage to shops and businesses in America. This was what Truman needed for his novel, some crazed fan becoming obsessed and inspired by the plot and committing a copycat crime, perhaps. Something like that would get the ball rolling for sure, but if no one was reading the damned thing, how the hell was it going to happen?

Sitting there in front of his PC, frowning at the poor online sales figures, an idea began to take shape in his head. It was a preposterous idea, a stupid idea, an idea that simply couldn't happen, but it was an idea nonetheless. *How far am I willing to go for my art?* Truman wondered as he mulled this unthinkable idea over in his mind. *To what lengths am I willing to go in order to make my book a cult hit?* He'd put in the countless hours writing it, he'd endured the tedious task of editing it, he'd spent a large amount of money promoting it—was he prepared to kill for it?

***

The thought of risking a lengthy prison sentence, as well as ending an innocent person's life all for the sake of a book, would've been unfathomable for most people. But most people were not artists, not committed ones anyway, whereas Truman most definitely was. His art was an extension of his person, his purpose in life, his reason for lifting his head from the pillow each morning, and so as the days and weeks wore on this insane idea gained more and more credibility within him. It became so credible, in fact, that one afternoon he found himself sat over his coffee table, staring down at an assortment of menacing items he'd purchased from a shopping mall across town. Among these items were an eight-inch kitchen knife, a pair of leather gloves, a black balaclava, a small battery-powered clock and, of course, an old-fashioned lottery ball machine.

But he wasn't really going to use them. He left them on the table untouched, arranged like novelty ornaments in a crime museum, glancing at them before leaving for work in the morning and then chuckling at them when he arrived back home. There was no way he was really going to kill anyone. It wasn't in him to do so; he wouldn't know where to start. He was far too kind and humane to carry out such a barbaric act.

That's what he kept telling himself, anyway.

He was telling himself this, in fact, even as he crouched down on the grass in front of a rural cottage, trying to look for a way in. He was telling himself this as he gripped the handle of the long knife with a gloved hand, trembling with anticipation. He was telling himself this as the cold night air stung his eyes through the exposed holes of the balaclava.

The country house had been chosen by the lottery machine after attaching some random addresses to the balls, and it just so happened to be out in the sticks, out in a farming town west of the city where stray sheep and horses roamed freely—chance had smiled upon him.

The lit-up windows of the cottage threw thick yellow beams of light out across the long grass, and Truman watched as a middle-aged woman pottered about inside her living room. Once he was satisfied that she was alone, he checked his coat pockets to see if he had everything he needed. In his breast pocket he could feel the casing of the small clock, in his outer pocket he could feel the freshly-printed copy of his novel that he'd ordered a few days before, and in a tiny zip-up pocket in the lining of his coat he could feel the two lottery balls he'd placed there earlier.

He was good to go.

A shivering, blubbering form lay upon the bed, a weeping mess curled up in a defensive fetal position. Twenty-four hours had passed since Truman's bout of murderous insanity, and most of that time had been spent sobbing into his pillow and biting his fingernails down to stumps.

As soon as he arrived back home, he burnt his clothes, gloves, and balaclava in the back garden and then scrubbed his body with a sponge under a hot shower for thirty minutes straight.

But he still felt filthy.

If only he could've scrubbed away his memory of the previous night. Scrubbed it all away, instead of being subjected to the incessant mental slide show behind his eyes, the slide show of butcheries carried out with his own hands.

The blood.

The blood that spilled from the arteries of the woman's neck had been so thick and viscous he could still smell it, despite the shower, and the sickly sound of steel tearing soft skin rang in his ears like a demented melody. And that still wasn't the worst part. Removing the woman's eyes with the tip of the blade was the worst, the thing that scarred him the most. It was awkward, tricky work, each one coming out like a soggy grape on a tender stalk, turning to mush in his gloved hand as he pulled it free. And then came the lottery balls—it had been like pressing marbles into pulpy fruit.

By the time he'd left the cottage, the woman had been reduced to a sliced cadaver slumped in a wicker chair, the ticking clock resting in her lifeless hands.

'What have I done?' he whimpered, rocking to and fro on his sweaty mattress. He wasn't a killer; he was a timid, unassuming writer who said hello to his neighbours and put coins in the donation box at the local supermarket. He'd gotten carried away with a desperate idea, a bout of lapsed sanity and judgement.

But this is for your art, Truman. Don't forget that.

And indeed it was. There was still a part of him, a tiny section of him deep in his core, that was hoping he might get away with it and see his book sales increase. It was possible. There was still a chance that his life might be transformed forever in a good way, if he could just control himself and hold his nerve. A copy of his book was in that old house a few feet away from the mutilated corpse, and if the press got wind of it there'd be an unending supply of publicity for his writing.

But the work was not yet done.

There was another layer of mimicry to be carried out, another section of the book to be replicated in order to lead people to the crime and create the required sensationalism. The Lottery Killer led people to his victims using complex puzzles and riddles, and so that's what Truman needed to do next.

In for a penny, in for a pound.

The Lottery Killer always set up a string of clues in different places, and he always set up the last one first and first one last, just in case anyone found the first clue and followed it before the rest were in place.

With this in mind, Truman jumped on a bus and travelled back to the rural town where he'd committed the crime. The vehicle rolled to a halt at bus stop number 18, and he lingered until all the other departing passengers had wandered off down the street.

Once he was alone, he walked over to the glass-covered map of the town that was displayed inside the bus shelter and began to unscrew the glass panel with a pocket screwdriver. Then, using a felt-tip pen, he drew a circle around the area where the dead woman's house was. Using the screwdriver again, he replaced the glass panel and put everything back how it was.

With this part of the puzzle in place, his next port of call was the zoo.

Zoos were of particular significance to the protagonist in Truman's book. Zoos were home to various creatures of chance, various creatures of a natural lottery. In a certain chapter of the book, the Lottery Killer breaks into the monkey enclosure of a zoo and leaves a cryptic symbol. Truman now had to do the same. And this could not be done during daylight hours for obvious reasons, hence the reason he was hurling himself over a tall iron fence under a pitch-black sky.

A zoo was a strange place at night. Wild cries and chirps emanated from countless dark shadows, a million tiny voices all rattling the cold air with their guttural pitches and primal screams. Truman crept along the walkways and paths, mindful that there was likely a warden or security guard on the premises somewhere. He knew this particular zoo well enough to know where he was going, and before long the recognisable squeals of monkeys could be heard up ahead in the gloom.

This is insane, he thought as he reached the primates' den. They were lashing around at his presence, and their pungent odour wafted out through the holes of the plexiglass wall. Was he really going to do this?

This is for your art, Truman.

After a quick look around, confirming that no security personnel were present, he pulled a pair of bolt cutters from his bag and went to work on a lock on a steel door, which led into the enclosure.

Snap!

The monkeys went wild, perhaps believing it was time for a late-night treat. In he went, regardless, into the shit-covered saw-dust and furry bodies, carrying a can of black spray paint in his newly-gloved hand. Long tails lashed and whipped inches above his head, branches swayed, leaves fell, but he ignored the mayhem and ran straight for the rear wall of the enclosure.

The golden ratio symbol is hard to draw in the dark, especially when you've got wild animals humping your leg and hanging onto your shoulders, but Truman did quite well despite the circumstances. He also managed to write a poem underneath the symbol, and when it was all finished it looked something like this:

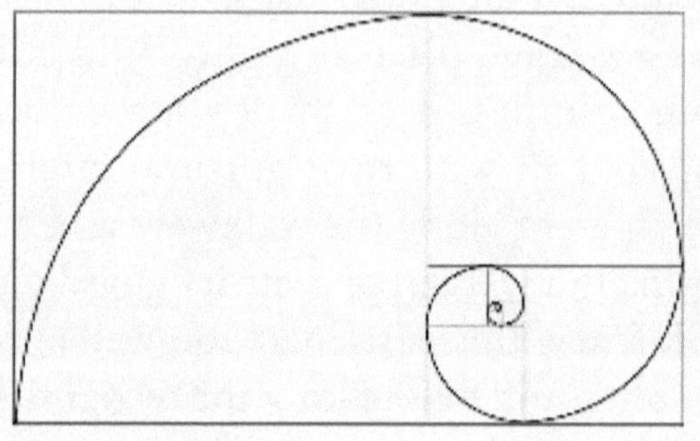

I'm big and red, you sit on me
Sometimes at the top
But don't stay on me for too long
Or else you'll miss your stop

Truman had enjoyed writing this scene into his book, although as he was leaving the zoo he wondered whether the clue might be a little bit too cryptic for most people to crack. In his book, a school teacher visits the zoo who knows that the golden ratio is 1.618, and he then works out that the poem points towards the number 16 bus and bus stop number 18, but would anybody crack the code in real life?

Only time would tell.

The last—or first—piece of the puzzle was completed just before dawn, and it was the easiest one of all. After hopping over yet another iron fence, he entered a huge communal park a couple of miles from the zoo and taped a different poem to a tree that he'd written by hand on a piece of paper:

> *You have to crack this code*
> *Or else my plan will fail*
> *And nobody will see*
> *My art I try to sell*
> *So run along right now*
> *With sweat and tooth and nail*
> *To see our furry friends*
> *Our cousins with the tails*

Content in the knowledge that scores of joggers and dog walkers would soon fill the park, and at least one of them would see it, Truman finally went home to sleep and wait.

And wait, he did. Then he waited some more. And after that, he waited even longer. He went to work, listening to the radio news channels as he packed and sealed boxes, and then he came home and watched the news channels. He became a kind of media junkie, feasting on newspapers, magazines, and channels every day, looking for an indication that his work of art had been discovered, but there was nothing.

Maybe the old cottage was too remote, he wondered. Maybe it was too hard to find. Or did he simply dream the entire thing? Had he become so obsessed and psychotic about making his novel a success that he'd hallucinated an entire series of events? No, that was absurd. He'd done it. He killed that woman, and he left those clues around the town.

So where was everybody?

As the weeks went on, the whole entire fiasco began to resemble yet another frustration in Truman's life. Was his book simply destined to go unnoticed? Was his art condemned to complete obscurity no matter what he did? What exactly did he have to do to get people to read his fucking story? He'd reenacted some of the scenes in real life, putting his future in jeopardy in the process. Did he not deserve a few sales for this kind of dedication?

The online figures said no.

For some people, there's a limit to how much they can take. They can only endure so many knock backs, they can only suffer so many failures, and they can only tolerate getting slapped in the face a certain number of times. Eventually, when it became clear that his heroic, grizzly, murderous, Herculean efforts were never going to get noticed, Truman became resigned to the fact that his dream of becoming a cult author just wasn't going to happen. There came a time when a person had to move on, change outlook, pursue another avenue in life.

And so, that's what he did.

He got a new haircut, replaced his wardrobe, cleared out his notepads, deleted his files, got a new job, and did his very best to pretend that none of it had ever happened.

Many years passed. He grew older, became more seasoned, more mature, and made some plans to save money and move away somewhere warm. The atrocity he'd carried out during his younger years diminished into a blurry memory in an unused corner of his mind, a confusion that sat on the dividing line of fact and fiction. He was pretty sure that he'd done it, but not completely so. Now and again he thought about it, hazy flashbacks skimming along his consciousness like snippets from a movie he once watched, but it was all detached and removed.

And then things changed.

He was on a lunch break one day, resting in a roadside diner after delivering parcels for a courier company he'd been working for for a while. Sat a table by the window, he absently sipped coffee and stared up at a hanging TV above the counter. The TV was tuned in to a news channel, and a bold headline lit up across the screen that almost made him choke on his beverage:

'THE HUNT FOR THE LOTTERY KILLER'

His veins turned to ice.

Trying his best to calm down and conceal his panic from the other diners, he quietly listened to the report. It appeared that somebody in the city had committed a murder almost identical to his own, including the replacement of the victim's eyes with lottery balls.

His hands trembled, and his breath came in short gasps. The news report raised a number of urgent questions: Who committed the crime? Was the murder inspired by his murder? Was the murderer familiar with his book? Was there a copy of his book at the scene of this new crime? If so, why wasn't it included in the news bulletin? Would the police link this new murder to him?

Truman's mind spun like an overloaded washing machine. His world, his life, was once again turned upside down.

There were only three possibilities that Truman could think of. One: somebody out there had bought his book and copied the MO of the protagonist. Two: someone had found his old victim at the cottage and, for whatever reason, had copied that. Three: some crazed lunatic had randomly come up with the idea of killing someone and replacing their eyes with lottery balls.

The third option was too improbable to give any credit to whatsoever, and so Truman soon dismissed it. That left the first two, and there was really only one way to find out which one it was.

He would have to revisit the old house.

***

Travelling back to the old country house was foolish, he knew it was, but he had to know what was going on. He could've sat tight, of course, and waited for the police to do their investigating, but he could sense that it was all going to lead back to him in some way. A plan was now needed, and he wanted to be one step ahead of everyone else.

Getting there was easy enough, and after walking down a series of narrow streets and lanes, retracing his steps from that fateful night long ago, a vast meadow opened up in front of him. The meadow looked different in the light of day, and as he trampled across it he wondered whether the old house would even still be there. But, low and behold, as he ventured farther out it came into view in the distance.

It sat in an overgrown corner of the field like a mouldy tombstone, a forgotten relic of a time gone by. Long grass covered its base, moss sat on its remaining windowsills, and its flimsy roof looked as though a strong gust of wind might blow it away. Standing before the house after all this time, Truman felt like he was staring into the weathered face of an enemy, a foe that wouldn't go away.

Apart from a couple of horses grazing the grass out in the distance, there was nobody around. And so, with trepidation coursing through him, he stepped up to the flaking front door and prepared to enter.

The foundations of the building creaked and whined as Truman stepped through its decaying interior, the wooden panelling and remaining window panes voicing their surprise at his unexpected return. The air was dense and musty, but he could see an archway up ahead along the lower landing. He was pretty sure that the living room of the house was through there, and so he crept towards it.

The living room door was open, and its interior slowly revealed itself one inch at a time with each delicate step that Truman took, like a panoramic photo spreading outwards. The wicker chair came into view, its weaving resembling a baggy, scraggy nest of twigs, and perched upon its seat was the dainty, delicate frame of a human being. A blind behind the chair allowed slitted beams of light to penetrate across the room, and this faint illumination was enough to reveal the fine details of the rotted corpse.

Truman stood frozen a few feet away from the chair, trembling from the absurdity of what he was seeing. From his particular viewpoint the head of the carcass resembled a cartoon character, complete with oversized bulbous eyes staring out from their sockets. Perhaps his shock was unwarranted, though, for what else did he expect to see? But still, the sight of the plastic lottery balls sitting inside the dried sockets of the skull filled him with outlandish dread.

The body clearly hadn't been touched or moved in any way. Clothes still covered most of it, wispy strands of grey hair fell from either side of the cranium, and brown claret stains covered the floor. The hands were withered and spidery, curled out from the frayed cuffs of an ancient blouse, the nails hardened to brown crust. Buried underneath this tangle of nails and fingers was the clock that Truman had placed there years ago, and again a surge of unwarranted shock bolted through him when he noticed it.

But there was something else, too, some unconscious element to this scene that did warrant a feeling of shock, some detail that raised his guard, although for a long time he couldn't quite place it. He let his gaze flit over the body some more, going up and down from the face to the hands and back again, and then, like a lightning rod from nowhere, he suddenly knew what the oddity was.

The clock was still ticking.

He'd placed the clock in the woman's hands over a decade ago, so how on Earth could it still be ticking, he wondered. Squinting down at the thing, he watched the second hand move around, completing its circular voyage across the numbers as though it obeyed an unknown set of physical laws.

Baffled and spooked, Truman once again raised his gaze to the face of the dead lady, as though she might be able to shed some light on the subject. Her face carried an expression of utter lunacy, the lottery balls bulging from the dried eye sockets like fungal growths. Her stare was mesmerising, however, magnetic in a horrific way, and then, going against all logical and rational thought, she spoke.

'Back away!'

A voice, as clear and bold as day, appeared to emanate from the woman's mouth. Truman jumped like a small child at a fairground, his lungs collapsing, his brain trying to make sense of what was happening.

'I said, back away!'

This time he was able to properly locate the source of the noise, and it didn't come from the woman, it came from behind him. Turning on his heel, he was confronted by a small cluster of people blocking the doorway, all holding weapons of some description. *Police officers. They've finally caught me.* That was the first thought that sprinted through Truman's muddled mind, but, after a few seconds passed, he could see that these people were not actually holding weapons at all—they were holding books.

He backed away from the corpse.

'Who are you?' said the person closest to him, a slim-faced man with mousy blond hair.

'I'm... I'm, err...' Truman racked his brains for something to say, some lie that would hopefully be accepted, but then he happened to notice what book the man was holding. It looked familiar. *Very* familiar. He then looked over at the others, down towards their hands. With rising dread, he realised that they were all holding paperback copies of *The Lottery Killer*.

Clearing his throat, he reordered his words and changed tact: 'I was just admiring my handiwork over there.'

The group—consisting of an oddball mix of men and women of various ages—gaped at him in quizzical disbelief. Every single one of them wore an identical mauve gown with gold emblems printed across it, but before Truman could fully make out what the emblems were, the front man piped up again.

'*Your* handiwork?' he said, dubiously.

'Yes,' choked Truman. 'My work.'

The small crowd mumbled and gazed across at each other.

'Do you really expect us to believe that you're the original Lottery Killer?' spat a young woman, clutching her book defensively.

Truman paused for the briefest of seconds, hoping dearly that his bold approach would pay off. 'No,' he said. 'I expect you to believe that I'm the original Lottery Killer, *and* the author of the book you hold in your hand.'

A long gasp rang out from them all.

'You're the author of the sacred script?' said the blond man.

'Yes,' confirmed Truman, trying to look as authoritarian as possible.

After some mumbling and murmuring amongst the group, the man looked him up and down and said, 'Prove it.'

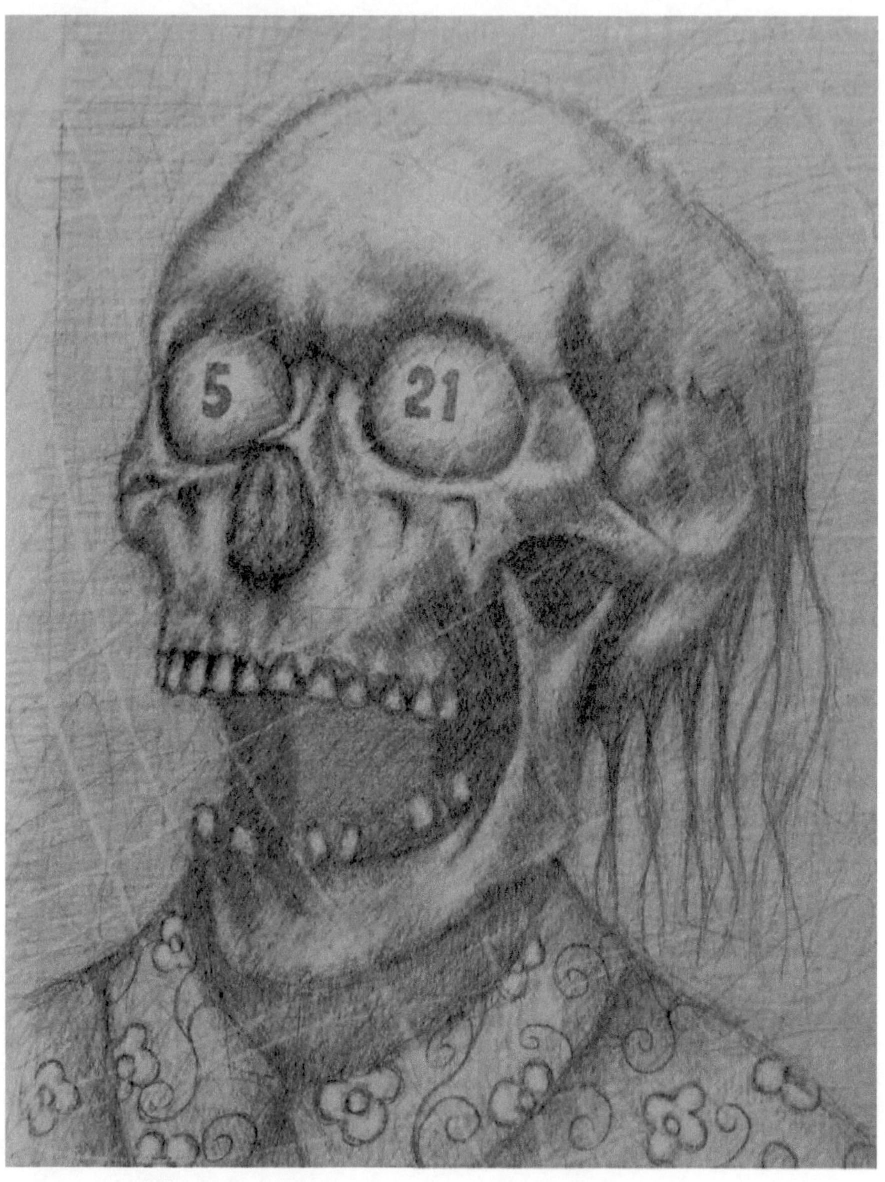

Ticking. Tick, tock, tick, tock. An incessant ticking seeped into Truman's ears and permeated his brain. The air was filled with a thousand ticks and a million tocks, and he could focus on nothing else. He was in a room upstairs in the house, perched on a high chair, and everywhere he looked he could see a clock. There were clocks on the walls, clocks on the shelves, clocks on a dusty table by the corner, and there was even a clock in his own hands that'd been placed there by one of the gowned cultists.

The chair he was sitting on was more like a throne. It was on an elevated platform at one end of the dank room, ornate and elaborate, and positioned in such a way that he could observe the rows of kneeling worshippers in front of him. The armrests of the chair had decorative spherical stops at the end, chromium lottery balls engraved with two-digit numbers, the headrest was clock shaped with real working hands, the cushioning was mauve with clock and number emblems printed on it, which turned out to be identical to the pattern printed on the worshippers' gowns, and, high above his head on another shelf, a paperback copy of his novel was on display in a reverent manner.

Proving his identity hadn't been too hard. He'd answered question after question about the plot of his book, describing the various characters in detail, and he'd even fully described the clues he'd left at the bus stop and the zoo and the park over a decade ago. By that point, the worshippers were almost won over, but the final test came when he was handed a piece of paper and a ballpoint pen.

At the opposite end of the room, hung on the wall in a gold frame, was the original poem that he'd left in the park that day. To truly prove his identity he'd been required to write the entire poem again, word for word, in handwriting that matched the original. The cult members had watched on in rapt silence as he did so, then once it was done they studied the end product like a bunch of crazed scholars crowding around a sacred document.

The handwriting matched, of course, elevating Truman to lofty heights.

By all accounts, logically speaking, Truman should've been happy and content. The one thing in life that he'd always wanted, his ultimate craving, was to have a cult following, and now he had one. But this was not the way he'd envisioned things to be.

He wanted to leave. He wanted to rise from the decorated throne and run out of the house, to dart across the meadow towards safety, but...he couldn't. The atmosphere in the room, the tenseness, the over-alert look in the eyes of the kneeling followers—it all spoke volumes. They would never let him leave, not now. He was invaluable to them, cherished, sacrosanct, and on top of this they also knew his own murderous secret.

The rest of his days were set in stone, and he knew it. His future was bound by the pages of his book, and forever he would be held hostage, trapped in the warped embrace of his zealous cultists.

Be careful what you wish for.

NOSTALGIA

She went out on a drug binge, one she couldn't afford
Then found herself bedbound, stuck in a hospital ward
At first she flipped and panicked, fighting with all her might
But then she saw the doctor, and he wished her a pleasant goodnight

Dr. Clingwill went from bed to bed, checking the patients' drips and dressings. The small ward was calm and quiet apart from the bleeps and hums of the machines, and the gentle rattling of the windows from a breeze outside. He was almost done for the day, his duties nearly completed; there were just some final tasks to be taken care of before he could leave and make his way home to the other side of Rachton.

A bandage had begun to peel away from an elderly man's shoulder, and he stuck it back down with some surgical tape, his ocean-blue eyes full of focus and intensity as he did so. Another patient on an adjacent bed was dribbling from the side of his mouth, and he leaned over to him and wiped it clean, his touch delicate and precise.

From certain angles Dr. Clingwill could be described as handsome, in a traditional, perhaps old-fashioned sense. With his white jacket and stethoscope, his combed brown hair and smooth face, he certainly looked the part. The only thing that tainted his clean image was the fact that he maybe tried too hard to look tidy and presentable, his manicured look giving off a sense of desperation and effort to the observant viewer. His parted hair had an unnatural tint to it, the after-effect of some off-the-shelf dye, and his pearly-white teeth were obviously caps.

In terms of work ethic, though, the man was exemplary in every way. A sick day was an alien concept, lateness didn't exist, and professionalism oozed from his every pore. The medical profession ran through his veins and flowed through his blood, and nobody could take that away from him.

Once he was satisfied that his ward was in order and his patients were in a good condition, he washed his hands at a sink by the wall and then made his way over to his office on the same floor of the hospital. Not one single worker passed him on the way, no nurses or surgeons brushing past him along the corridors, but this was all simply a testament to his excellent work and dedication. While he was on the job, nobody else was needed—that's how he saw it, anyway.

It took him twenty minutes or so to write up his notes. Sitting there behind his desk—the desk that'd been in the same spot for longer than he cared to remember—he wrote a brief report for each one of the bed-bound patients, cutting no corners with any of the details or figures. Once they were done, he filed the papers away in a filing cabinet behind him and gathered his personal belongings together, finally allowing himself to end his shift.

After climbing into a rather dated-looking car, Clingwill inserted a plastic cassette tape into the stereo and pulled out of the hospital grounds, locking a security gate behind him. The huge hospital building shrunk and receded in the rear-view mirror as he accelerated away from the complex, its dark brickwork and black guttering merging together in the distance.

Passing motorists turned their heads as the doctor cruised along the main roads of the town, the automobile's retro shape and design catching most people's attention. Clingwill seemed oblivious to this, however; sat upright in the driver's seat with his manicured hands gripping the wheel, he was somewhere else entirely, lost in the sounds of a bygone decade as the tape played.

It didn't take that long for him to get home, around forty minutes or so, and when he reached his leafy street he pulled up on his driveway and killed the engine. Trudging across the stones, he made his way to the front door. He knew that his wife would be at home, and after fumbling around with his keys for a while, working the stiff lock, he poked his head around the frame and called her name.

'Katherine?'

A faint reply came from the living room, and so he then proceeded to hang up his coat and take his shoes off in the hallway, his presence in the house declared. Running a hand through his immaculate hair, he breathed a satisfied sigh of relief at having completed another day.

The doctor's home was as neat and organised as his office, and his wife, Katherine, was sitting in her usual place on the cream sofa, her face creased in concentration as she pondered some crossword puzzle on her lap. Clingwill walked over and sat next to her, planting a kiss on her cheek, before asking her about her day.

The two of them lived a quiet life together, but they were happy. They'd been through some ups and downs in recent times, what with Clingwill's job, but they'd fought through them all and now, after a lot of hard work and determination, arranging and rearranging, things were back to how they were. By eight o' clock the two of them were huddled together, engrossed in a film flashing out of the chunky TV set, a decades-old mystery drama which they'd both seen more than once, lost in the grainy, familiar scenes.

Zoe was staggering along the pavement, her steps erratic and sloppy. She'd just emerged from the dingy tower block behind her in the distance, after overindulging once again with her shady group of acquaintances. Life was uncertain right now for young Zoe. A year ago her parents had kicked her out of the family home for quitting college and smoking drugs in the house, and since then things had gone from bad to worse. Her occasional social drug use had swiftly turned into a regular habit, and the mild homegrown cannabis had progressed into stronger stuff like MDMA and cocaine. She'd turned into something of a lost soul, sleeping on sofas and floors, no real direction to her life, and the few decent friends she once had now avoided her and didn't answer her calls, tired of lending her money and not getting it back.

Funding this habit of hers was obviously a continuous problem, and she'd run up a number of debts with several people. With twice as many enemies as friends she should have been slowing down, but on the contrary her recklessness seemed to be escalating. Tonight, she'd settled one of her smaller debts by dropping to her knees in front of a particularly horny dealer, hence the reason she'd gotten her fix despite having an empty purse.

The problem she faced now was finding a place to crash for the night, but she knew someone who would probably let her sleep at their flat as long as she shared her packet with them, and so it was there that she was headed. Progress was slow, though. Teeth grinding from the MDMA, nose blocked from the lines she'd sniffed from the coffee table up in the apartment block, the terrain in front of her was a dark blur punctuated by streaks of orange street lighting, all swirling in an unfocused whirlpool in front of her dilated pupils. Her legs felt like thin slices of jelly, wobbling and struggling to support her weight, and after bumping into a lamppost she finally buckled and fell across a grass verge that was damp with cold dew drops and patches of urine. She was conscious, but only just, dimly aware of the succession of car headlights tearing past on the main road a short distance away. When one of the cars stopped, apparently to see if she was okay and check on her, she felt as though she were sinking down into the wet mud and grass, slipping away into a chemical haze. The last thing she heard before oblivion were the words: 'Let's get you to safety…' before her eyelids dropped shut like lead weights.

***

When her eyelids finally opened again it was no longer dark, nor was she outside. She was staring up at a high ceiling with rows of long lights positioned in straight lines, the plastic casings yellowed and cracked with age. It took a long time for her eyes to adjust to her new surroundings, and even then things were still fuzzy and hazy around the edges, as though she were viewing things through a fish-eye lens.

She was stretched out upon a bed, that much she could tell. The bed was soft but not too soft, with a wafer-thin sheet covering her tender body, which she could just make out in her lower peripheral vision. *I'm in a hospital! Oh, no! What happened? What did I do last night?* Her groggy mind worked itself into a frenzy trying to recall the events of the previous evening, but all it could come up with was vague snapshots of drinking and bingeing in some rundown apartment somewhere.

She tried to get up but couldn't. An invisible force pinned her body to the bed like a ten-tonne weight, and this horrible realisation caused panic to ripple through her. She then tried to scream but found that her voice wouldn't work, either, no matter how much she strained to make a noise. In fact, the most she could do in terms of bodily function was turn her head left and right by about an inch on both sides, and so she did this continuously, trying to take in as much of the strange room as possible. A large window space to her right-hand side revealed a cloudy sky with a line of treetops poking their heads above the sill; over to her left, the square outline of another bed was visible, with a scrawny foot hanging out from under the edge of the sheets; on the other side of the room, in front of her, was a closed door. The air was stagnant, dusty and, apart from a series of dull bleeps coming from somewhere behind her, quiet. *Okay, calm down. Keep calm. I probably just passed out last night or something. I was drinking, taking things. A nurse will be along in a minute, and they'll tell me exactly what happened.*

With focus and willpower she forced herself to relax and close her eyes again, while she waited for a staff member to come along.

Zoe was pulled out of a light sleep by the sound of a creaky door hinge. She was dimly aware of a tall man entering the room, sheathed in white, his lean figure moving its way towards her bed. As she regained consciousness again she was greeted to the sight of two piercing blue eyes looking down at her lovingly, the warm gaze instantly putting her panicked mind at ease. A doctor was here, at her side with a clipboard clutched in his left hand, and a faint smile creased the sides of her mouth in relief.

'You're awake,' the man said, with a healthy dose of compassion in his voice. 'I was starting to get a little bit worried about you.'

'Wherrr... Wherrr... am...' Zoe wheezed.

'You're in an intensive care ward, my dear. You were in a terrible state last night, intoxicated and dehydrated to a dangerous level, and you were brought in here after collapsing in the street. Don't worry, though,' he winked, 'I've dosed you up with vitamins, and your drip is slowly re-hydrating you.'

The doctor looked down towards her arm as he said this, and for the first time Zoe realised that a plastic tube was indeed attached to the inside of her elbow. She couldn't turn her head enough to see it, but she could feel it there as a dull sensation against her skin.

There was a million things she wanted to say to the doctor now that he was there with her. She wanted to ask him what hospital she was in, whether anybody had been informed of her admission, and how long she'd be there for, but...she couldn't. The strange paralysis that'd taken over her body was still there, pinning her down to the mattress, preventing even her vocal chords from working properly. She also wanted to ask him why she felt so immobilised, so incapacitated, but all she could manage to do was make a few incoherent gurgling noises.

'Don't you worry about a thing,' said the doctor, noticing her inner struggle. 'You're in safe hands; everybody gets the best treatment in my ward.'

'Uurrrgghhh...'

'Get some rest. You need it,' he said, finally turning away from her to tend to other patients.

Zoe was screaming inside, yelling at him not to leave her, but nothing except a series of groans and grunts came out of her chapped lips. She lay there, wriggling and squirming again like a worm on a hook, while the doctor paced around just outside of her view, whistling and scribbling notes on his clipboard.

———

'See you tonight, dear!' shouted Dr. Clingwill, stepping out of his front door and strolling towards his car. While the old engine was warming up, rattling away on the driveway, he checked his dyed hair in the rear-view mirror and adjusted his tie. Some presenter was harping on about a rise in missing persons on the radio, a few tramps and tearaways disappearing, so he pushed the cassette tape back in and replaced the irritating noise with nostalgic music. Once the car's angry noises and grumbles had died down, he reversed out onto the road and pulled away.

The first port of call for Clingwill on this particular morning was the chemist, where the owners knew him by face and by name.

'Ah, hello, Doctor!' said a portly man behind the counter as he walked in.

'I'm here to pick up my order,' said Clingwill, beaming his warm, clean smile.

'Yes, of course,' replied the man, searching behind him for a white paper bag with the relevant label. 'How's things over at the practice?'

'Very well, thank you. Just fine.'

The chemist nodded and smiled at Clingwill's brief reply, and left it at that. He felt rather sorry for the doctor, as did a lot of people around town. The closing of the old hospital had been devastating for him, costing him his job, and without being offered a position at the new, grand Rachton State Hospital, he'd been forced to open up a private general practice in a different borough somewhere. This upturning of his life couldn't have happened at a worse time, either, what with his wife's health issues back then.

'Here are your supplies, Doctor,' he said, placing the bag on the counter. 'I'm glad things are going well again.'

'Have a wonderful day." Clingwill grinned, playfully, his clean-shaven mouth curling up into a humble grin.

With a courteous nod he turned and left, the bag of medicine dangling from his moisturised hand.

The signs and notices by the side of the road were invisible to Clingwill as he turned right into the small lane. The words "Trespassers will be prosecuted" existed, but at the same time didn't exist. The colours and letters flashed before his eyes, but his brain swept them away some place hidden. The steel notices existed in some realm somewhere, some other dimension, but not the realm of his focused, conscious mind. The same held true for the tall, barbed-wire fence and the iron gates that he unlocked every day upon entering the hospital grounds: he knew that they were there, existing somewhere in solid form, but he refused to acknowledge them as part of his world. From Clingwill's point of view, the entrance to the hospital looked just as it did during the peak of his career, back when everything was okay.

As soon as he'd absently opened the big gate and entered the grounds, the original, council-issued padlock snapped and disposed of long ago, he drove down the long, overgrown road towards the staff car park. He had no trouble finding a parking space, what with the entire lot being a messy, weed-ridden, pothole-covered patch of abandoned tarmac, and after switching off the engine and gathering his bags, he stepped out of the creaky car and whistled his way to the crumpling hospital entrance.

The corridors were not caked with mouse droppings as Dr. Clingwill walked proudly along them in his polished shoes. The elevators were not out of service, the staff rotas and health information posters were not peeling away from the walls, there was no stale odour in the air, and the stairwells were not eerily silent. As the doctor made his way up to his office carrying his bag of restricted drugs and medicines, he was back in his heyday, back in a time when everything was pristine and working. The corridors shone under his feet, the elevators pinged every two minutes as patients and visitors stepped in and out of them, the walls were gleaming with fresh paint, the air was thick with heat and disinfectant, and nurses greeted him as he ascended the stairs to the first floor.

The patients needed checking, so he didn't take too long slipping on his white coat from the hook on his office wall and dating a new report sheet. He was out in the ward in no time at all, clipboard and drugs clutched neatly in his fingers, eager to carry out his doctorly duties to the best of his ability. The six patients moaned and fidgeted on the row of beds before him, all in need of more shots and tablets. Most were men, shaggy and unshaven fifty-somethings, but at the end of the row, over to the left, lying relatively still under the sheets, was his newest patient: a teenage girl. Clingwill didn't like to indulge in favouritism as it went against his professional obligations, but someone had to be tended to first, so he chose her, telling himself that she was currently more needy than the others. Her face came alive when she saw him approaching, the glazed expression lighting up a little.

'Hello, Zoe,' he said, walking gracefully over to her side. He didn't need to look down at the clipboard to see her name; he'd already memorised it from the ID card in her purse. 'Let's give you some meds and vitamins. You look a little gaunt.'

As he prepared a syringe on a small steel table next to the girl's pillow, outside of her field of vision, the moans and groans from the adjacent beds rose in volume, his presence in the room causing a stir among the impaired occupants. *They're calling out for me, bless them*, thought Clingwill, as he filled the barrel of the syringe with clear fluid. *I'll sort them out. Nobody gets neglected on my shift.* Then, looking down towards the girl's pale face, he said, 'This won't hurt a bit.'

The girl's arm twitched and shook under his grip, her thin muscles tensing and flexing, but she was too weak to fend off the shiny tip of the needle that was sliding into her skin.

'There, all done. Calm down now, dear. You're in no condition to start moving around just yet.'

Placing her arm back under the cover, he moved away and flitted from bed to bed, humming and whistling some old tune as he checked catheters, took temperatures, crushed tablets, and recorded figures on his clipboard. Walking around the grey, dimly-lit ward, tending to the sick and needy, he was in his element, the harsh realities of the outside world all nonsense and insignificant.

Absorbed in his jobs and his duties, evening came around quickly for the doctor, and after filling out the last of his paperwork, he conducted one last walk around of the ward, carrying out some final checks before clocking off for the night. With pride he concluded that his patients were in a fine condition, recovering steadily from their ailments, and after washing his hands he wished them all goodnight and turned towards the door. Over his shoulder, as he was exiting, he even heard the girl praising him, murmuring her appreciation.

'You please me, Doctor! You're the best! You're the best!'

'My pleasure, dear.' Clingwill chuckled. 'Now, do get some rest.'

With a courteous nod he closed the door, then made his way home.

'Don't leave me, Doctor! Come back! Come back!' croaked Zoe, as the doctor was preparing to leave.

She knew what this meant: the clipboard was in his hand, the rubbish had been cleared away, the sun was low and pink outside the cracked window—he was leaving for the night. *What kind of doctor are you?* she thought. *What kind of...hospital is this?* As Zoe watched him lingering by the door, trying to gauge his thoughts and intentions, his combed hair glowing in the warm sunset rays seeping in from outside, he simply smiled and told her to get some rest.

After the door clicked shut, she was alone once more with the rest of the comatose patients, the sky getting darker by the minute.

———

Zoe knew now that the medication, whatever it was, lost its potent edge as time went on. She'd been lying on the bed for what seemed like an eternity, listening to the gurgling and spluttering of the men in the adjacent beds, and she guessed that it must've been somewhere around five a.m. The bleeps of the monitors behind her were like the incessant sounds of a broken record, a continuous playback tugging at the strings of her sanity, and she felt as though she could take no more.

Movement was coming back to her hands and feet, just as it had yesterday, and if she focused hard enough she could actually lift her head from the pillow. The grunting forms on the neighbouring beds seemed older than her, apparently lacking the energy and curiosity to question their surroundings much, but she was different; she was fighting back. Straining against the invisible hand pinning her down, the unknown concoction flowing through her veins, she tried with all her might to get her limbs moving again. She had to wrench her body out of its induced slumber, snap it back into action, and she began by pounding her heels against the springy mattress, building up a steady motion. The more she did it the easier it got, and once her legs felt alive again she moved onto her arms.

Eventually, she was able to move her hands around enough to remove her drip, and then, with a herculean effort, she pulled the bedsheet away from her and swung her legs off the edge of the mattress, dangling them a few inches above the floor. She then leapt from the edge of the bed, conducting the manoeuvre like a parachute jump, and braced herself for the landing. The hard ground sent shockwaves through her sleepy bones, but she managed to stay upright and began walking around in her thin gown, using the moonlight from outside as a visual aid.

The plug sockets and switches in the room were in working order, she knew this because she'd observed the doctor using them, so she went straight for the light switch. The ward was suddenly illuminated in warm, yellow light, and she gazed around, dazed, taking in the various oddities surrounding her. The corners of the room were filthy with dust and grime, the bed frames rickety and old, but the equipment lying around looked functional. It was like someone had swept out an old garden shed somewhere and set it up to look like a hospital ward, imitating the real thing. The dozing patients were lined up in front of her, eyes closed, oblivious to the sudden brightness of the room. The unmistakable stench of body odour emanated from them in a huge wave, and they all seemed to have the crusty look of someone taken off the street—rather like she had, she thought, rather uneasily.

Traipsing across the room like a tranquilised gorilla, she made for the corridor outside with an aim to do some exploring. She was confused, baffled, and completely unsure of whether the hospital was genuine or not. The dirty state of the place told her it wasn't, along with the doctor's long disappearances, but...it just had to be. Why would it be anything else? It occurred to her that her drug-addicted mind might simply be playing tricks on her again, like it often did, so she was in a state of complete indecisiveness.

There was a stairwell in the corridor, and she lurched towards it, holding on to the bannister for support. Her body was like a dead weight that she had to drag along, each step painfully slow and exhausting, and by the time she reached the ground floor she had to stop and sit down. Pale moonlight shone in through an array of cracks and windows, highlighting the flaky paintwork on all of the walls. The medication—as well as the drugs she'd taken the other night—still governed her bodily system, and it took everything she had to get herself back up to her feet. The sound of rats scurrying around accompanied each step, but she ignored it all and headed towards what looked like the hospital entrance.

She let herself fall into the big set of double doors and they burst open, the cold night air chilling her skin. The overgrown car park stretched out before her like a hostile wasteland, the lumpy terrain completely uninviting. The treetops she'd glimpsed from her bed were just visible in the distance, a row of black spikes pointing up towards the chalky moon. There was no way she was going to be able to make it out of the hospital grounds, not in her present state, and she fell into a heap by the open doorframe and wept at the sheer insanity of the situation. *This is crazy! What am I doing?* She couldn't relax in the hospital due to her dark suspicions, but at the same time she felt ridiculous crawling around the corridors in the early hours of the morning like this. What was she to do?

Out of nowhere, an idea dawned on her: *Phone. Shouldn't a hospital have a phone?* There was obviously an electricity supply *to* the building, so if there was a phone somewhere it'd presumably work. And, also, it occurred to her as she slumped in the doorway, if there was a phone in the building it'd probably be on the ground floor. But who would she call? And, for that matter, what would she tell them? She hadn't the foggiest idea where she was, that was the point, so how could she lead anyone here? The answer to this conundrum, she didn't know, but she was going to try her luck and look for a phone anyway—what else was she going to do?

With a rough plan of action in mind, she dragged herself back up yet again, with the speed and agility of an eighty-year-old woman, and began to search the dingy ground floor for a phone.

It took her fifteen minutes or so to find one, a wall-mounted setup with a chunky keypad, and it hung from a wall opposite a locked storage room of some kind. A faint hum came from somewhere beyond the locked wooden door, a deep vibration that she could feel under her bare feet. *A generator, perhaps?* It sounded like one, but she couldn't be sure, so she ignored it for the time being and focused her attention on the phone.

The earpiece was covered in dust, so it was a shock to hear a dial tone coming from it when she picked it up, but it was there. Rather tragically, there was only one person's phone number that Zoe knew completely off by heart: her main drug dealer's. This was the last number she wanted to call, but the only one that she could. But what would she say? What would she tell him?

A second idea then occurred to her: the doctor, presuming he was real, must have an office somewhere, probably close to her ward, and if she was lucky she might find something in there with his name and address on it, or maybe the address of the hospital. Putting the receiver down, she headed back to the stairs, pulling her drained body back up to the first floor.

As she'd suspected, the doctor did indeed have an office on the first floor, just beyond the ward. The stuffy little room had the feel and look of a museum exhibit, like a preserved dwelling of some long-dead historical figure, everything laid out as though it'd been that way for years. This worked to her advantage, however, because after a very brief search through some of the neatly-organised drawers she found exactly what she was after: a letter with a personal name and address printed along the top of it. *So you are a real doctor*, Zoe muttered to herself, staring down at the words: Dr. Allen Clingwill.

The horrible feeling of stupidity and humiliation ran over her again at this realisation, and she felt foolish standing there in the office dressed in just her hospital gown. The doctor was legit, and if he was legit that meant that the hospital was legit too, and if the hospital was legit that meant that she was crazier than she thought. *Shit! What am I doing? I'm fucking losing it!* Was it the medication playing tricks on her? Was it the alcohol, cocaine, MDMA, or whatever else she'd put in her body over the last few months? Was she actually rummaging through the doctor's office in the middle of the night, shuffling around like a confused dementia patient? She wasn't sure of anything anymore, but she knew that she had to do something, so, closing the drawers back up and leaving the office, she made her way back downstairs towards the phone.

In the silent murkiness of the downstairs corridor, leaning against the wall with the phone pressed up against her ear, she tentatively dialled the number for her main dealer, Chris, then closed her eyes and tried to compose herself. After a few rings, a gruff voice echoed down the line, and she opened up to him.

'You what?' he shouted. 'What do you mean you don't know where you are?'

'Chris, please just listen to me!' she croaked. 'I can't speak for long, but I just need you to check someone out for me.'

'Check someone out?'

'Yes, the doctor. And...and maybe follow him.'

'What've you taken, Zoe? I'm in no mood to listen to you rambling on about—'

'Chris, please! I know it sounds crazy, but...I don't know, just drive over to this address and...and go from there. I need to do something! I'm desperate! I'll call you back later on this number, and you can tell me what happened.'

'But—'

'And maybe you could try to trace this phone number. Look up the area code or something.'

'What do you think I am, a fucking private detective?'

'Chris, I can't explain it! There's just something not right about this place! This is all I've got. Can you do it for me?'

'Why should I? Why should I help you out? You owe me money, for fuck's sake.'

After a moment's hesitation, Zoe said, 'I've got your money! I've got it here with me.'

'Bullshit!'

'No, Chris! I have!'

'How the fuck have you got money? You've—'

'I borrowed some a couple of days ago.'

'From who?'

'It doesn't matter, just trust me. If you do this for me, you'll get your money tonight.'

'If you're lying... If I do this and it turns out that you're lying...'

'I've got your money, Chris. I just need to find out where the hell I am.'

After another few minutes of pleading and exchanging details, she ended the call and stood quietly in the dark hospital corridor, not quite knowing what to think or feel. Gradually, out of a deep weariness, she lowered herself to a seated position under the phone and waited, hoping that Chris would do as she asked him to.

The black sky was turning purple as Chris sped down the road in his BMW. He was tired after a night of driving around, delivering wraps and packets, but the small line he'd just sniffed was helping him to stay awake and alert. What on Earth was he doing? He had a name and address, and he was heading over there to...what? Spy on someone and follow them? It was insane. The girl owed him a lot of money, however, and that was the only thing driving him forward.

The built-in sat-nav display was declaring an ETA of three minutes, and so the tracksuit-clad, muscled young man turned the stereo off and took note of his surroundings. The street was spacious and quiet, with big trees lining the pavements and large gaps between each brick tenement. He was in a posh neighbourhood, and the sight of it immediately flicked a switch somewhere in his tearaway, petty criminal mind. Burglary was not out of bounds within his social circle, and this particular street represented an untapped goldmine.

The house he was there to look at was straight ahead on the curve of the road, and the first thing that caught his eye was the old car sitting on the driveway. It wasn't dated enough to be vintage or classic, but it wasn't new enough to be a common sight, either. It kind of dampened his hopes a little bit as it wasn't exactly a display of wealth and money, but still, the big house looked as though it might've been harbouring some valuables nonetheless.

It was still dark enough to walk around without being noticed, so he parked up a decent distance away from the detached house and strolled towards it, making an effort to look as inconspicuous as possible in case anyone happened to be peering out of their windows at this early hour. Reaching the driveway, he looked down at the car with a look of pitying disgust. A pile of cassette tapes were neatly stacked in a small crevice by the gearstick, and a ripped, bent tax disc was displayed in the window that wasn't even needed anymore. *What kind of twat drives a car like this?* thought Chris, whose own vehicle looked luxurious and futuristic in comparison. A wide-brimmed hat and a pair of laced gloves sat on the passenger seat, clearly belonging to a woman. *Some old codger and his wife*, he thought, with a sardonic grin. The last thing he noticed in the car before moving on was a pile of blankets on the back seat, along with a cushion. Unsure of what to make of this, he simply shook his head and headed over towards an iron gate by the side of the house.

The gate separated the front drive from the back garden. It was locked, but he climbed over it with ease. Chris wasn't planning on breaking into the house right now, not at this hour on his own, but he did want to scope the place out a little. As soon as his feet touched the ground, he could see yellow light spilling out from the rear of the house, illuminating a large patch of dewy grass across the long garden. Somebody was awake. Looking in through a side window, using the glowing light and a series of reflections, he worked out that the lit-up room was a kitchen–dining room area, with two figures sat at a table. *An early breakfast, perhaps? Probably*. Elderly people often got up early, and besides, the time was getting on.

With the intention of taking a quick look at the locks and windows, Chris crept along the shadows as stealthily as he could, his eyes darting around everywhere. Once he was done scoping out the side of the house he moved around the back, quickly sizing up the large back window, which looked out across the garden. The locks and handles looked semi-secure, not cheap but not impenetrable, either, and with a knowing smirk he swiftly turned to leave, shooting the briefest of glances through the big window towards the two occupants at the dining table as he slithered away back towards the gate.

After two paces he paused, however, frozen mid-stride.

The image of what he'd just seen through the glass flashed in his tired mind like a chilling snapshot, a surreal slide, forcing him to stop and acknowledge it. He'd clearly been awake for too long, burnt the candle at both ends for too many nights, because otherwise what he'd just seen through the window would've been real. His muscled arms tensed as he crouched there by the big dining room window, nervously bracing himself for a second viewing. He had to look again just to prove to himself that he wasn't going mad or, conversely, to prove that he was. Positioning his head by the bottom corner of the window frame, using the leaves and branches of a potted plant for cover, he looked back in at the couple sitting at the table.

China teacups were set out in front of them, along with a pot of steaming brew. Plates of toast and jam were scattered around here and there, with an assortment of cereal boxes and cartons of milk to go with them. A lean-looking man with dark hair, presumably the one Zoe had mentioned, was chatting away to his wife in between mouthfuls of toast, his voice a muffled vibration on the other side of the glass. Rambling on, lost in the throes of conversation over breakfast, he laughed, smiled, and giggled at the woman opposite him.

And it was the woman's face that'd brought Chris back to the window for a second look.

At first glance she looked extremely tanned and weathered, like she'd just got back from a holiday abroad perhaps, but upon closer inspection it became clear that her skin's imperfections ran a lot deeper than that. Her cheekbones were barely concealed by the dried-out, leathery strips that ran over them, the glow of the bulb above the table reflecting against their protruding contours. Her nose was flat and stubby, and a pair of shrivelled-up lips curled sickeningly around black gums like pieces of torn, mouldy orange peel. The eyes—or eye sockets—were little more than dusty holes in the front of a crumbling cranium, gazing across the table at the rambling man with total and utter indifference. A few wiry strands of white hair were pulled back across her peeling scalp, secured with a flowery hairband, and her dainty body sat upright with a stiff, rigid posture.

Looking in through the window at this peculiar scene, this odd, chilling scene, the young man's own body took on a similar stiffness, although his was due to terror, not decay. He was glued to the spot, unable to look away from this clothed corpse who was being spoken to by a deluded man across the table from her, drinking tea and eating mouthfuls of food. But then, just as he was starting to notice additional details from within the house—the retro-patterned wallpaper; the antique lampshade above the table; the chunky TV set in the corner, throwing grainy light from its thick screen; the silver fork that'd been carefully placed in the woman's fingers, the thin digits clasping it like rusty strands of wire—a noise rose up from somewhere out in the darkness, causing the man at the table to turn his head.

'Tanner? Is that you, boy?'

It took a few moments for Chris to register the implications of what was happening. There was a dog nearby, somewhere out in the garden with him. He could've sworn that the noise had come from somewhere else, some other garden a few rows down, but the man's reaction to it stated otherwise. He was now rising from the breakfast table, edging around the dining chairs towards the back door, and Chris turned and bolted with such explosive energy that he tripped over his own feet. He'd hardly made it two metres from the back window and he was flat on his face, elbows and knees stinging from the hard concrete.

He was still in this position when the door opened behind him, the slender figure of Clingwill leaning curiously in the frame. Chris knew he was standing there due to the silhouette cast along the ground, the new light from the doorway shining a rectangular glow across the floor with his outline in it. This new light illuminated different sections of the garden that were formerly obscured, lighting up shadows around buckets, pots, and dirty shovels that were sitting around the place. Enveloped in this bright light, Chris suddenly found himself looking into the eyes of an Alsatian dog. It'd been there all along, sitting by a wall behind him, hidden by the mauve shadows of the early morning twilight. It'd made no sound when he'd illegally entered the premises, no growls or barks, no whines or yaps, and for good reason: every crevice of its hollowed-out face was teeming with ants and bugs. Its entire head and body was as stiff and motionless as the woman's at the dining table, its dark patches of hair matted with cobwebs and bits of stone and gravel. Yellow teeth protruded from a wrinkled snout in a permanent, silent grimace, hundreds of tiny insects swarming over them like dark bloodstains.

'Tanner? What have you found?'

The man's words sent icy stabs through Chris's body, the seemingly sophisticated tone of his voice somehow adding to the horror of what was happening. Clambering up to his feet, he scarpered with more determination this time, the fear rooted within him adding spring to his step. He was back over the iron gate with the speed and agility of an Olympic hurdler, sprinting down the street towards his car without as much as a glance over his shoulder.

It wasn't until ten minutes later, flooring his car a few miles down the road, that he realised he'd lost his wallet.

Parked up in a quiet lay-by a safe distance away from the house, Chris lit a cigarette to calm his nerves. What he really wanted was a line but the wrap of powder was in his wallet, wherever the hell it was. Well, he knew exactly where it was: it was back in that garden. That wasn't a good thing at all, as there was a bank card in the wallet with his name on it, along with the packet of drugs. *Could the police charge me with that?* he wondered. *Damn right they could.* With anybody else the answer would've been no, but Chris had pissed the police off one too many times, so they'd definitely find a way.

He was looking out towards the road, puffing on his cigarette, mulling this strange situation over in his head, when his mobile phone began to ring. The number Zoe had called him on earlier flashed across the screen, causing his piercing ringtone to echo around the interior of the car. Zoe—the girl who never paid what she owed, the girl who always seemed to bring trouble wherever she went, the girl who had him driving around in the early hours of the morning even though she was in debt to him. His wallet—an incriminating piece of evidence that could potentially get him locked up again—was back at that house because of her. If it weren't for her sending him out on a stupid little mission, he wouldn't have lost the bloody thing. He thought about not answering it, just letting it ring and ring, but then, with a sadistic glint in his eye, a better idea occurred to him.

'Hello,' he said, pressing the green button and putting the device up against his ear.

'Chris! Chris, it's me! How... How did you get on? Did you find the address?'

Chris thought for a moment before answering, his mind on overdrive. Waves of guilt rushed through him, but his annoyance with the girl, along with her bad history, overrode it. He also had to do this; he had no option. Reporting the man to the police would inevitably lead to them finding his wallet and his drugs, and they'd never let him get away with that. There was no way he was going to go to jail for a nuisance customer like Zoe.

After taking another long drag of his cigarette, blowing smoke out of a small gap in the window, he said, as calmly as he could muster: 'Yeah, I found it.'

'And?... What—'

'It looks normal to me, Zoe. Just an old couple living in a suburban house.'

'And what about—'

'This phone number? I looked it up online. It belongs to Rachton State Hospital.'

'You mean I'm—'

'You're in the state hospital; there's nothing to worry about. Now go and get your head down and get some rest. It sounds like you need it.'

'But...are you sure? I mean, this place looks—'

'Stop panicking and get some sleep. I'll collect my money another time.'

A brief silence hung over the line, and then, after a moment, the girl's voice rose up again like a confused whisper.

'Well, if...if you're sure.'

'I'm sure,' said Chris. And then, gritting his teeth, he added, 'Goodbye Zoe,' before ending the call.

Out in a forgotten corner of the town, the old derelict hospital sat in the dim morning light like a crumbling relic. As the sun inched its way above the horizon behind it, pink-orange rays shone in through the rotting window frames, making faint forms and objects visible within the building.

Apart from a small gathering of birds lined up on the roof and guttering, flapping their wings and tilting their heads, and a few foxes scurrying around the empty car park, the only movement to be seen across this desolate tableau was a small figure walking along inside the ruin, traipsing past one of the illuminated window frames like a dark shadow or ghostly apparition.

Reaching a bed, they tiredly climbed up onto it, the sun's rays outlining their movements as it crept higher up into the sky. After sitting there for a moment in a state of apparent confusion, gazing outside towards the overgrown wilderness, they slowly leant back and put their head against the pillow, ready for sleep.

MUSINGS ON HUMAN EXISTENCE

A baby's thrown into this world of chance
Another life, another living branch
Rolled into the hardy game of life
No choice, no say, a random toss of dice

For every man alive, there was a million
Who lost the race and sank into oblivion
But did they really lose by not existing?
Being spared of all life's ills and heavy lifting?

Trapped inside the ruthless realm of time
And stuck inside a rotting human mind
One has to ask the question, time to time
Is life a gift, or just an awful grind?

DEADLY DISPOSSESSION

He made a kind decision, a very noble one
It was a hard thing to do, because he loved his son
Letting go wasn't easy, and he started to crack
That's the reason why, he wanted the bloody thing back!

PART ONE

It's Friday night. The sound of distant partying makes its way through my apartment window, and into my cluttered living room. Drunken laughter and boozy banter can be heard down on the street two floors below, as groups of drinkers stagger from one pub to the next. My night has no such enjoyment in store, however. My night, the night of Eric Harris, is going to be far from enjoyable.

Old, flaking cardboard boxes surround me as I sit on the floor, trying to sort through the endless clutter that I've brought back from my parents' house. It's been a month since the accident, and I've hardly made any progress at all in clearing out the old family home. The shock, the pain, the trauma, the sudden loneliness...it's all just too much.

All four of us had been in the car that night: me, my wife, and both of my parents. We were on our way back from a weekend break. It was only a cheap, all-inclusive deal at some small hotel on the coast, but we all enjoyed ourselves. It was late on Sunday night, and I was driving back. Everyone else was dozing in the car, and I was trying my best not to do the same as I sped along down the motorway. I've been wondering whether I was actually asleep too when the car in the next lane lost control and skidded into us, because I can remember so little about it. There was a mighty thump against the door as we collided, that I recall, but before that everything's kind of hazy. After that awful thump, it was all screeching tarmac and shattered glass, bits of plastic dashboard flying through the air. The tormenting part of it all, the bit that nags away at my mind the most, is the fact that my wife, mother, and father all survived that initial impact; it was the oncoming traffic from behind that killed them.

The car was compressed to half its size. I only managed to survive due to the angle that the cars hit us. The doctors said I was lucky. Looking around me tonight, alone in the silence of the empty flat, I have to say that I beg to differ. The driver who caused the accident didn't hang around, and the eyewitness accounts are all very sketchy and unspecific. The most the police have to go on is that the car was green, possibly a hatchback. Nothing too promising.

It's kind of ironic that I was the one who survived that night, considering my chequered medical history. I'm certainly no stranger to hospitals. In fact, I've pretty much been in and out of them all my life. By the time I was twelve years old, I'd already spent more time in hospitals than an average person does in their lifetime. It's my heart, you see. Well, I suppose I should say it was my heart. I underwent heart surgery at that tender age, after struggling through my childhood years with serious problems and complications. The doctors said that heart transplantation was my only option, and the ten-inch scar across my chest is a constant reminder of that. Nowadays I pretty much have a clean bill of health, but I still can't help seeing the irony of me surviving when everyone else died.

So here I am, alone, picking up the pieces of my shattered life. I'm burdened with the daunting task of clearing out my parents' old house before putting it up for sale; hopefully, after that, I can attempt to build a new life for myself. If I feel strong enough, that is. I sigh with despair, like a balloon deflating. Either side of me I've got piles of old letters, bills, videotapes, DVDs, CDs, plates, clothes, ornaments, and countless other stuff that's been sitting up in a loft gathering dust for the last decade or so. A pile of paper sleeves catches my eye, and I'm drawn towards them. I can tell without even touching them that they're full of old family photos, and I also know that if I start flicking through them all I'm going to spend at least a couple of hours doing so, and won't get any work done.

'What the hell?' I mutter.

The photos do nothing to ease the pain. Every single one of them is simply a grim reminder of what I once had—of what I've lost. Bent, yellowed pictures from years ago pass through my fingers, pictures that I'd long forgotten about, stages of my life lost to the sands of time. Strange haircuts leap out at me from faded snapshots in locations I don't recognise; outdated clothing makes me cringe and tingle with embarrassment even though there's nobody else here to see it.

They don't all feature me, of course. A thick stack of them are from my parents' wedding, and there are countless others of distant relatives I've never even met before. I find myself looking for more pictures of me and my mother together, something that I can keep in my wallet, maybe. An old Polaroid sticks out from the pack and I pick it up. It's a holiday photo. I remember this one well; it was taken in Tenerife. I was twelve years old, and my father had treated us all to a vacation after the stress we'd been through after my operation. There's a big rock formation in the centre of the page, and I'm standing on it, my mother looking up at me with a proud look in her eye. The haze of an afternoon sun simmers behind us, leading out towards the sea. How I wish I could morph myself into the picture, jump back into that carefree moment in the warm sun, somehow. Things were far from perfect back then, but they were a hell of a lot better than this. I carefully place it down on the floor beside me and continue browsing.

A picnic photo catches my eye this time, and this one also has both me and my mother in it. The two of us are sitting on a blanket in a park somewhere, a selection of plates, cups, and containers laid out around us. My father probably took the photograph, as I can see an extra pair of shoes on the grass in front of us. I look slightly older in this one, a couple of years, maybe. Studying the picture closely, it's clear that we were not the only ones in the mood for a picnic that day, as several other people are visible in the background. A trio of young students are sat to the left of us, beer cans in hand, an elderly couple to the right, and off in the background a lone man is sitting on a bench.

A strange sensation hits me when I see this man, a kind of unexplained familiarity. Studying this man in the background of the old photo, I feel as though I've seen him before. This in itself would've been enough to disturb me somewhat, but my discomfort is heightened even further by the fact that the recognition feels recent, like I've seen him somewhere else within the last few minutes. His features are fresh in my mind. He has an odd look about him. His face is grey and pasty, and a thick pair of spectacles circle his beady eyes like round frames. Mousy white hair covers his head.

A thought enters my head. It's a stupid thought, ridiculous even, but I can't help but listen to it. I go back to the previous photo, the one of me climbing the rock formation. I don't fully know why I'm doing it; it's more of a subconscious impulse, as if a deeper part of my mind knows something that I don't. This impulse obviously holds some merit, however, because a second later I see him. He's there, in the background of the first photo, this time perched on a rocky wall instead of a bench. My blood runs cold with a creepy, eerie terror. I compare the two photos, checking the face a few times, hoping dearly that I'm wrong. But my hope is short lived because there is simply no mistaking it—it's the same man.

My fingers tremble and the two photographs drop to the floor. The air in my living room feels cold all of a sudden, tense. It can't be right, it just can't be. The two photos were taken years apart in completely different parts of the world, so how could this random stranger be in the background of both of them? It's the stress, I tell myself, getting up to go and make a drink. This is, of course, the rational explanation, but as I wait in the kitchen for the kettle to boil, I'm neither reassured nor convinced.

The hot tea I've just brewed tastes good, and I welcome the warmth of it. Feeling a little calmer, I start flicking through the old photos again, and this time I'm specifically looking for the white-haired man. There are dozens of pictures, but I patiently sift through them, curious to see if I can find any more with him in them. Half an hour passes with no result. A multitude of pictures come out of the boxes, but he's nowhere to be seen in any of them.

It takes another forty minutes of searching before his face stares up at me again from one of the glossy surfaces, but this time it's clearer than ever.

This photo's pretty recent, and sharper, with more definition. It can't be more than two years old. Me and my ex-wife are smiling at the camera, sitting down in a restaurant across town that used to be our favourite. I remember the night well. This man, this spectacled man, he's sitting over on a table behind us, alone. He's looking away from the camera, his jaw set tight. This one really puts the hook in me, because it's so close to home. The restaurant is less than a mile away from my apartment, less than a mile away from where I sit right now.

I look closely at this one, real close. Everything about him is strange: the black glasses, the bushy eyebrows hanging over the top, the slate-grey skin, the brown suit that looks as though it's been worn a million times. A familiarity hits me again, but this time it's different. This time I get a feeling that I've actually spoken to this man at some point, interacted with him in some way. Now that I can see him clearly like this, his face is known to me, as though he's played a part in the structure of my life somehow.

I put this photograph with the other two, then continue searching.

Another hour passes by as I go through the boxes, flicking through every image I can find. A school photo works its way to the top of the pile I'm looking at, and a tremor runs through me as I look down at the printed image. It's a secondary school, end-of-year, class picture, and thirty or so students are all lined up, including me. A handful of teachers stand either side of us, arranged neatly into the composition. A mop of silver-white hair draws my eyes to it like a beacon, and now, I realise, I have a name to put to the face.

Mr. Crisp. The name springs up out of nowhere, like it's been waiting impatiently for an opportunity to rise to the surface of my mind for the last couple of hours. Mr. Crisp the supply teacher. How did I not realise this straight away? How did I not remember that face? That hair? He used to come into the school and teach us when others teachers were off sick, filling time by handing out crossword puzzles and word searches to twenty or so uninterested kids. He was as eccentric as they come, always erratic and on edge.

This revelation only deepens the whole mystery, though. Why is an old school teacher of mine lurking in the background of several photographs that've been sitting in my parents' loft for years on end? It's all too much for my tired, fragile head to take, and I wince as I look up at the clock on the wall and see how late it is. My bed is calling me, and I'm calling it. This riddle needs a refreshed mind to solve it, I decide, so I stand up and go to the bathroom to brush my teeth.

Standing in front of the mirror, I run through the possibilities. It simply wouldn't be feasible to put all of this down to a simple, innocent coincidence, that much is true, I acknowledge to myself. With this option lost to me, I turn to the tenuous hope that this whole entire fiasco might just be some fatigue-induced hallucination, something that'll cease to exist when I open my eyes in the morning. The idea is pleasant and soothing, and I cling to it dearly.

PART TWO

The last two days have been torturous. Some of the boxes have been cleared away now, but the pile of photos sit on my living room table, silently taunting me every minute of every hour. I've been thinking about reporting the issue to the police, but the more I consider it, the more futile it seems. No crime has been committed, and all I have are some old pictures. The uncomfortable scenarios that run through my head are enough to put me off going to the station: incredulous stares from overworked officers; smirks and giggles as I pull out the old, faded photos of me as a child; the embarrassment of walking out after being told there's nothing that they can do. The whole thing is too flimsy for the authorities to deal with, but on the other hand, it's too serious for me to ignore.

The only thing I really have to go on is the name. I figure there can't be that many people around with a surname like Crisp, so perhaps I can track him down on my own somehow. The local registry office, the public library, the employee records at my old school...all of these things are running through my head as I stuff the selected pack of photos in my bag and walk out the door, determined to find some answers.

Walking down the street makes me nervous. I feel exposed, naked, almost. The invisible weight of eyes and stares press down on me, and I hold onto my bag as though it's a comfort blanket. There's a bus that goes directly to the council offices, and I wait at the stop by the end of the road, glancing around me. The handful of commuters waiting at the bus stop keep their distance from me, and people walking past veer off towards the curb to avoid getting too close. It's at this precise moment that I realise how troubled and disturbed I must look, how noticeable and visible my stress must be to those in my close vicinity. I find myself wondering how I would react if I were to see myself in this way as a passer-by.

The bus comes rolling by after a few minutes, and the small crowd along the pavement try their best to get themselves lined up with the doors so that they can get on first. I'm the last to get on, and I awkwardly grab hold of the door rail and begin to heave myself up onto the big step. I'm halfway on the bus when I stop, frozen mid-stride, half my body hanging out of the big automatic doors. A strange colour catches my eye and I'm drawn to it, looking over towards it while I balance on the edge of the step. The colour is brown, a sickly shade of brown, and it comes from a blazer a man is wearing on the corner of the street. There's something about the blazer that demands my attention, some oddity, and then, when I see the grey mop of hair flapping around above it, I realise exactly what, or who, I'm looking at.

The loud, impatient voice of the bus driver snaps me out of my frightened daze, and I'm then forced to make a split-second decision to either step onto the bus and drive away in relative safety, or step off the bus and confront this apparition-like figure that stands fifty yards away from me on the corner of the road. Deep down, I know what I have to do. I jump off the bus and let it pull away, the angry, disgruntled faces of the passengers whizzing past me in a blur as it accelerates down the road, leaving me alone to face my demon.

Without a single word from either one of us we draw closer to each other, walking through the thick cloud of exhaust fumes the bus left in its wake. Our eyes are locked in a tense, mutual understanding; our bodies move in unison. Each second feels like a year as we edge towards one another, and I take in everything I can about him. In the flesh, Mr. Crisp looks even creepier. There's a desperation lurking under the surface of his grey skin, a beseeching expression carved across his weathered features. His presence is intimidating but not in an aggressive sense, rather an eccentric one; his posture and demeanour paint a picture of imbalance and unpredictability. He looks at me not with hate but with longing, behaving in the manner of someone meeting a long-lost relative they haven't seen in a while.

'Alex,' he whispers, coming to a gentle halt before me on the pavement.

It takes a few moments for the name to register with me, as I'm trembling all over and my head is a jittery ball of fuzz. Just as I'm about to correct him, however, he leans forward ever so slightly and continues, his voice raspy and high-pitched.

'I'm so glad you've remembered, so glad you're here again. Please come with me. There are so many things we need to discuss.'

'I'm not going anywhere with you,' I cry. 'You're going to tell me what the hell's going on, and you're going to do it right now! Right here!'

My outburst surprises him and he seems to switch gears, the tone and pitch of his voice altering as though he's now talking to someone completely different.

'Please come with me,' he says, this time with more calculation and control. 'I'll explain everything.'

'Who are you? Why have you been following me?'

'I'm... an old friend. An old friend of your parents.'

The mention of my parents arouses a fresh burst of emotion and I yell at him again, causing a couple of pedestrians across the road to turn their heads.

'An old friend of my parents? I've never even—'

Reaching into his blazer pocket, he pulls out a card, throwing me off kilter for a second and cutting off my words. He passes it over to me and I hesitantly take it, studying its yellowed antiquity. It's an old thank-you card with an outdated design, but I instantly recognise the handwriting inside. It's my mother's writing; the curves and strokes leap out at me from the stained paper. I look up at Mr. Crisp with a steely expression, demanding some kind of explanation.

'Just read it, and you'll see that you can trust me,' he says.

I read the card.

Dear Mr. Crisp, we could never thank you enough for what you have done, but please just know that we are forever in your debt for your kindness. We can only envy your warmth and generosity. If there's anything we can do for you, just let us know.

I still have no clear idea of what's going on, but after reading these words I feel as though I should at least hear Mr. Crisp out and listen to what he has to say. I hand the card back to him, loosening up slightly.

'Let's get away from here,' he says. 'We're making a scene.'

Taking a deep breath, I slowly nod and concede. We walk around the corner and away from the main road, leaving the noisy traffic behind us.

I'm sitting in the passenger seat of Mr. Crisp's car as he navigates the roads. There's a musty smell to the interior, but it looks fairly clean and tidy. A silence lingers between us, and I focus most of my attention on memorising the route we're taking.

He drives the way you'd expect an elderly man to drive: obeying every speed limit, indicating at every turn, stopping for every red light, etc. I feel fairly safe in the car with him, sensing no risk of any kind of traffic collision. Now and again, as he changes gears and steers the old car around corners, I surreptitiously study him from the corner of my eye. Judging by the deep creases in his skin and the frailty of his limbs, I reckon he must be in his late sixties at least.

We eventually turn into a quiet, leafy street, with neat-looking houses lining each side. With careful concentration he maneuvers the car onto a brick driveway, then finally cuts the engine.

'Here we are,' he says, smiling at me warmly through his thick black glasses.

After getting out of the car I look around, checking my surroundings for anything suspicious. Nothing seems amiss. A gentle gust of breeze blows leaves across the innocent-looking street, and the only real activity I see is a black cat stretching its arms and legs as it lays across a patch of grass. But despite the lack of any kind of visible threat, my pulse still quickens as I follow Mr. Crisp to the front door. It's too late to back out now, however, so I simply reassure myself by acknowledging the fact that I could physically overcome this man if I really needed to.

The house is decorated and furnished but it has an empty feel to it, and I can instantly tell that Mr. Crisp lives alone. A cushioned sofa sits in the corner of the living room with various shelves, wooden chairs, and ornaments positioned here and there. Everything I see has a dated look to it.

'Please make yourself at home,' he says, waving an arm towards the old sofa. 'Would you like a drink?'

'No thanks,' I reply.

Thankfully, Mr. Crisp keeps his distance, pulling up one of the wooden chairs to sit on.

'It must feel good to be back, does it not?'

'What?' I reply, startled.

An embarrassed look crosses Mr. Crisp's face, and he corrects himself.

'Oh, nothing, erm... Look, why don't we—'

'Why don't you start by telling me why you've been following me?' I interrupt. 'Why are you present in some of my family photos?'

'What photos, Alex?'

'What photos?!'

My hands are shaking as they fumble around inside my bag, but I eventually locate the paper sleeve and throw it onto his lap.

'Here! These photos!'

A warm smile appears on his face as he flicks through them, and it's only then that I realise he's addressed me by a different name again. Just as I'm about to ask him why, however, he starts muttering to himself.

'Oh, the memories. So many years ago now.'

'What do you mean? Why were you even there in the first place?!' I scream. I'm on the verge of losing it. The stress of the last couple of days, as well as the last few weeks, wells up inside of me, looking for an outlet. 'And why do you keep on calling me Alex?'

A look of concern crosses the old man's face, but only for a second.

'Let me show you something...'

His voice trails off before any name is uttered, but then he continues:

'...that'll make everything fall into place.'

He rises from the wooden chair and walks towards the door, beckoning me to follow. I do so, rising from the sofa and gingerly walking across the room. We go along the downstairs hallway, all the way to the staircase. The stairs creak under our weight as we both climb them, Mr. Crisp leading the way. The walls are lined with beige wallpaper, with faded floral patterns printed across it; it makes me feel dizzy as it skims past in my peripheral vision.

We make it to the upstairs landing, and he comes to a halt outside one of the bedrooms. The door is closed.

'Come on in,' he says, pushing the door handle down with one hand and adjusting his glasses with the other.

A strange smell hits my nose as the door opens. It's a dusty, stagnant smell, but there's something else there as well. Dirt. Soil, maybe. The curtains are drawn, but sunlight penetrates through an inch-wide gap, giving my eyes just enough light to adjust to.

After a moment or two, I realise that I'm standing in a child's bedroom. Curled, dog-eared posters hang from the walls with bits of tape, and an array of comic books and magazines litter the floor. It looks to me like a boy's room, but everything is faded and covered in a thin layer of dust. Standing there, surrounded by these delicate, untouched items, I actually feel as though I'm in a museum rather than a child's bedroom, and my body stiffens with fear and uncertainty. Mr. Crisp moves around the room, and I watch him, noticing the way he carefully steps over the old books and magazines as though they're sacred items.

He finally stops by a bed in the corner. It's a small, single bed with a thin duvet; it's too dark to make out the exact colour. There's not much light in this corner of the room so it takes my eyes another few seconds to focus properly, but when they do I let out a startled cry and take a step back. To my astonishment, a small form is visible under the bedcovers, a figure laid on its back. The arms and legs look skinny, withered, even.

'Who...is that?'

Through the dingy murk of the room, I see Mr. Crisp's lips curl up into a loving, adoring smile.

'It's you, Alex, my boy! It's you! You just need to...' His gaze drops down a notch, as though he's staring at my chest. '...get back in there.'

The room begins to spin and breathe around me as I realise who it is on the bed. Raising my hand to my chest, I feel the lump of my scar running down towards my abdomen, the pink raised tissue that formed after my heart transplant all those years ago. I'd been twelve at the time, and my donor had been roughly the same age.

Movement from the shadows snaps me out of my nightmarish train of thought, and I look up to see Mr. Crisp pulling back the covers on the old bed, exposing the skeletal form underneath. Dried skin clings to the arrangement of splintered bones, wrapping tightly around them like scraps of shiny leather, the only exception being the parts of the broken rib cage that stick out and reach for the ceiling. Further up the bed a skull rests on the pillow, two black sockets sunk deep into it. The mattress cover is sprinkled with clumps of some kind of dark substance, presumably soil from the boy's grave.

Slowly but surely, I'm backing away from the bed, trying to gain some distance from Mr. Crisp so that I can reach the door without him getting to me first. I manage about three steps before he notices what I'm doing.

'Come on now, Alex. Let's just get everything back in place, and things can go back to normal.'

'Get back! Stay away from me!'

He's edging towards me now, walking around the bed.

'I know that you can hear me, Alex. Don't let him control you.'

A reflection flashes up from where he's standing, caused by the beam of sunlight coming through the crack in the curtains. Mr. Crisp's hand then rises up to reveal a surgical scalpel blade, light and razor sharp. I scramble for the door in a frenzy, feeling the delicate pages of old comic books rip and tear under my feet as I go. I'm out of the room in no time, leaping back down the staircase two steps at a time. The front door comes into view just as Mr. Crisp's stumbling footsteps rise up behind me, and I lunge for it and yank down the handle. Relief washes over me like a cool, welcome breeze as it swings open, and I throw myself out onto the sunny driveway. I'm barely halfway across it when I hear Mr. Crisp's nasal voice from behind me, its raspy screech sending my hairs up on end.

'Be strong, Alex! Don't let him take you away from me!'

I need to see how close he is, so I turn my head and have a look. He's standing right there in the doorway, silvery hair ruffled and askew. His scrawny hand still clutches the chrome scalpel. There's a wild, possessed look about him, and in this fraction of a second, as I look back at him over my shoulder and gaze into those tormented, panicked eyes, I suddenly see him as a victim. I see the deluded, deranged soul that lurks within him, the man who lost his son, the man who lost his grip, the man who lost his sanity, the man who became so lonely and desperate he committed his entire life to following me around, even going as far as somehow getting a part-time job at a school I used to attend. But the thing is, the real truth of the matter, that he hasn't actually been following me around all these years; he's been following this heart that thumps away in my chest, the last remaining piece of his beloved son.

Seeing him in this sympathetic light alters my view of him, but it doesn't make him any less dangerous, so I continue running across the driveway towards the road. As I do so, I see one last thing that causes the remaining pieces of this twisted puzzle to fall into place.

The car is still there in front of the house, Mr. Crisp's car, and there's a huge dent in the off-side wing. I'd failed to notice it earlier, but it's there, big and deep. Another thing I'd failed to notice was the actual colour of the car—or the significance of its colour. Mr. Crisp's car is green. This fact consciously registers with me for the first time as I'm halfway across the drive, mid-stride. The official police report of the car accident that killed my family included a description of a green car. I need no further clues to convince me that Mr. Crisp was the one who ran us all off the road that night, no further evidence is needed, but it comes, anyway.

A broken streak of red paint runs along the inside of the dent. My old car, the car I was driving on the night of the accident, was this same shade of red.

My legs ache due to the vicious pace at which I'm sprinting, but I don't slow down, not one bit. There's a main road not far up ahead in the direction that I'm heading; I remember it on the way here. My only plan is to flag down a police car, maybe. Beyond that, I'm literally running wild, concentrating only on widening the distance between me and the house at any cost.

Heads turn in the street as I run, curtains twitch behind windows, lampposts and garden gates whizz past me in a blur. I stop for nothing, ignoring small alleyways and side roads, leaping over curbs and drain covers like they're not even there.

This goes on for several minutes, running through the suburban streets, but then, out of nowhere, I'm overcome with a sudden sensation of flying. It's completely unexpected and bizarre. My legs actually leave the floor, and a vast blue sky takes over my field of vision. For the briefest of seconds it seems as though some kind of bird has swooped down and lifted me into the air, but then the illusion shatters when I feel my body drop and smash down onto rough tarmac. The towering bulk of a double-decker bus then looms over me, the frightening sight punctuated by the sickening sound of screeching brake discs. A scream and a gasp rises up from somewhere, then heads and faces appear around me in a circle as I look up in a daze. Phones are pressed against ears, and details are exchanged.

Seconds pass, then minutes, then, very gradually, the distant sound of sirens fills the air. I'm aware of all of this, but only dimly, and by the time the ambulance arrives I feel completely detached from my surroundings.

Bright lights pass over me, the fluorescent glare glowing behind my closed eyelids. When I eventually open my eyes, I see the ceiling panels of a hospital corridor, accompanied by the bleeping sounds of medical equipment around my head. Masked nurses chatter to each other as they push me along on the stretcher.

I've been in many hospitals over the years, but this time it feels different; this time feels like the last time. I feel separated from everything, including my body, sinking down into a black hole. I have one last thing to say to the world, however. There's one last piece of information that I need to share, and I try hard to fight against the deep fatigue that's pushing me down so that I can spit it out.

Even the simple task of opening my mouth takes a herculean effort of willpower and determination, though. My lips are heavier than lead, and my tongue feels like a sleeping boulder at the bottom of some deep ocean. I groan and moan, cough and splutter, frantically trying to put a sentence together so that I can inform the nurses that a crazed, deranged man is on the loose and that the police need to be called immediately. But the words won't come, only a long series of incomprehensible gurgling sounds, and to make matters worse, after a few moments one of the nurses interprets my noises as a call for some kind of pain relief, and she lowers a big plastic mask over my face, which blasts me with gas and air. Everything around me turns into blurred patches of colour, the colours merging and swirling together, and then, as I sink lower and lower, the colours fade and disintegrate into nothing.

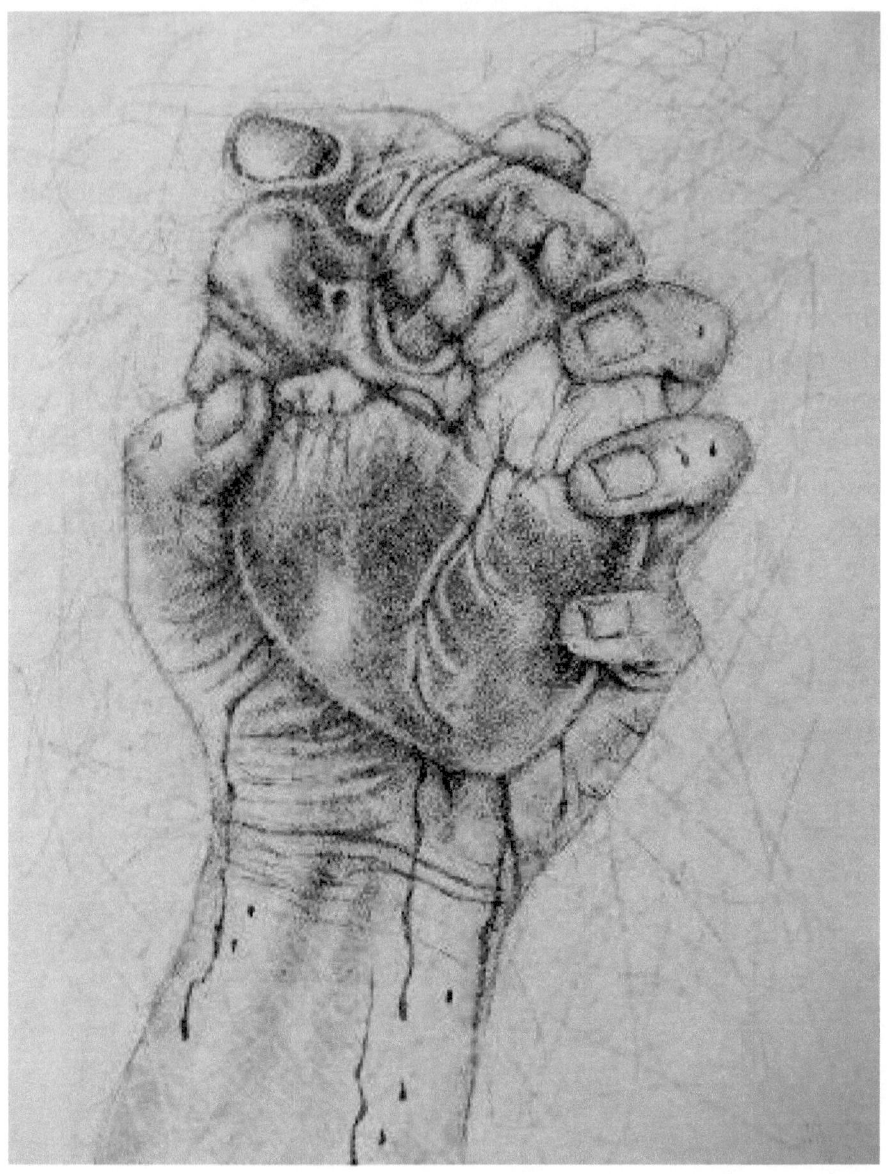

PART THREE

Down near the ground floor entrance of the hospital, a small family waits in anticipation. When the elevator pings and the doors slide open, they all clasp their hands tightly around each other, and the mother begins to weep. A wheelchair emerges from the lift, pushed along by a nurse, and perched on the seat is their beloved relative, a young man recovering from his major operation.

The last few months have been hard for the family, especially the parents. With a shortage of donors in the area it began to seem like their son would never get a new heart, but a recent fatal traffic collision involving a bus and a pedestrian created a change of circumstance for them. Finally, after waiting for so long, their son had been given the transplant that he'd needed.

A brief exchange is made between the nurse and the family: reminders about medication to be taken, information about dates and times of follow-up appointments, and then final pleasantries and farewells.

Outside in the car park they all help him to get into the car, then fold up the wheelchair and put it into the boot. Two minutes later the car pulls out of the hospital and accelerates down the road, joining the stream of traffic. The atmosphere in the car is happy and joyous, the conversations filled with optimistic plans for the future. They are all lost in the emotional moment, so lost, in fact, that no one notices the car that's tailing them, mirroring their every turn. So engrossed are they in this happy, emotional moment that not one of them notices this green car with the dent in the wing and the crazed, bespectacled man hunched over the steering wheel.

PUSSY PAYBACK

It was a weekday morning
The boy got up for school
His face was bright and smiling
But soon his mood would fall

With Mum distraught and crying
And Dad with spade in hand
It soon became apparent
The day was going bad

The house was full of mayhem
The neighbours fighting back
And what was it all over?
A small suburban cat!

W hen young Clayton first woke up and opened his bleary eyes, it seemed like an ordinary Tuesday morning; nothing seemed amiss whatsoever. Climbing out of bed, he walked to the bathroom to take a shower, and then put on his school uniform. Cereal was his usual breakfast dish, and he made his way downstairs to make some.

Halfway down the staircase, however, a light sobbing could be heard. The sound was coming from the living room, and so he bypassed the kitchen to go and investigate.

For reasons unknown to anyone, except perhaps the architects of the suburban housing development, the living room of Clayton's childhood home was situated at the back of the house, looking out onto the back garden, and so the first thing he noticed as he entered the room was his father out on the back lawn with a shovel in his hand. Then, a moment later, he looked down towards the sofa where his mother was weeping into a handful of tissues.

'What's wrong?' he asked, pausing by the door.

'It's Jasper,' whimpered his mother, wiping her nose. 'Jasper's died.'

Mixed feelings washed over young Clayton as he stood there in his blazer and tie, feelings of profound confusion and loss. Jasper was, or had been, the family's pet cat, a mischievous little feline with black-and-white markings covering its agile body. After absorbing this unexpected news, he looked back out towards the garden and noticed a rectangular patch of flattened dirt by his father's feet.

'What? But...how?'

'We don't really know,' cried his mum, Luna. 'I found him out by the curb about an hour ago. He might've been run over or something.'

Young Clayton wasn't really of a disposition to start crying himself, he wasn't very expressive in that way, but as he watched his father patting down the damp soil outside, a genuine sadness welled up inside him. He'd been very close to Jasper, or as close as it was possible to get to a cat, anyway. Jasper had been a part of his upbringing, an element of his childhood, and now he was gone.

The thought of going to school after this awful discovery wasn't very appealing at all. How could he focus on schoolwork in this state of mourning? However, he doubted very much that his headmaster—or his mother, despite her distraught state—would accept the death of a pet as a valid excuse for a day off, so he did his best to gather himself and then finally went to the kitchen to make breakfast.

'Don't worry, luv,' said Luna, as he was walking out towards the back garden to leave. 'We'll all remember him.'

'Yeah, I know,' said Clayton, still feeling glum.

'Try to have a good day,' she said, with a forced smile.

Clayton nodded and plodded along towards the back gate, resigned to the fact that it definitely wasn't going to be a good day at all. Halfway down the garden path, however, he heard a loud noise. The tall wooden gate began to shake under the weight of something clambering over it. Then, in a flash, a furry creature appeared at the top edge, jumped down, then came walking down the path towards him.

It was Jasper.

Clayton had never seen a ghost before, nor did he believe in them, but as the recognisable form of his deceased cat came sauntering along the path at his feet, he had to ask himself whether things had now changed.

'Mum!' he yelled. 'Mum, it's Jasper!'

His mother appeared, looking confused. 'What is it?'

Clayton pointed down towards the cat, alive and healthy, and his mother turned white.

To be fair, it was quite an easy mistake to make. Nobody knew that there was a woman on the block who owned a cat with identical markings to those of Jasper. Her house was far enough away for her to be unacquainted with Clayton's family, and her cat, for whatever reason, had never strayed away that far before. However, easy mistake or not, they now had somebody else's cat buried in their back garden.

When young Clayton finally left for school, he couldn't help smiling.

The day went smoothly enough for him. When he told a couple of his friends in class what'd happened, they both laughed, and he could relax in the knowledge that Jasper was safe and sound after all.

Late afternoon, over the dinner table with his parents, Clayton looked out into the garden and remarked, 'Huh. Isn't it weird that we've got someone else's cat buried in our back garden?'

There was an awkward silence.

His mother finished her mouthful of food and replied, 'Oh, no, it's not there anymore. We dug it up and put it back out by the curb.'

Gobsmacked, Clayton said, 'You did what?'

'Well, what were we supposed to do?' she said defensively. 'We couldn't just leave it there.'

After a moment's thought, the boy had to admit to himself that his parents had been faced with a rather tricky predicament. Should they have left the cat buried under the lawn, knowing that its owner was out there somewhere looking for it? Or should they have dug the furry corpse back up and put it outside to rot, giving the anonymous owner a chance to find it, but also exposing its mangled body to everyone else unfortunate enough to stroll past it? It was a tough one. Maybe they'd done the right thing.

As this was discussed over the table, Jasper purred contently on the arm of the living room sofa, oblivious to the hilarious mix-up he'd been involved in.

And unbeknownst to them all, on the other side of the estate, at number thirty-seven, a sour-faced lady was burying her deceased kitty under the dimming afternoon sky, thoughts of cold, hard revenge fuelling her tired arms.

It was very early in the morning, but the woman at number thirty-seven was awake and alert. Anger had made sleep impossible, and she could think of little else other than the cruel crime that'd been committed against her. What on Earth had they done to her poor cat?

She'd seen them carrying him out across the car park yesterday, dumping his lifeless body down by the curb like it was a worn-out toy. What a horrific sight. And what a peculiar family, too, she mused. The pixie-faced woman, the lanky husband with his small eyes, and the ginger son with those pointy red ears. The thought of any one of them interfering with her cat sent a shiver down her spine.

And what did he do to deserve it? Did he climb into their garden and piss on their roses? Did he steal some of their cat's food? She'd probably never find out, but she'd get her revenge, nonetheless.

An eye for an eye, a cat for a cat.

Jasper had always been an early riser, roaming the estate every day at the crack of dawn. A pompous creature, he strolled along the pavements and alleyways as though he owned the land itself, searching for some kind of food.

Mice were fair game, as were certain birds, and if he was especially hungry he'd even take a bite out of an earthworm. And, of course, a random bowl of unattended cat food was akin to a jackpot win on a fruit machine. And it was for this reason that when he approached the open gate of number thirty-seven—a gate that was normally locked—and saw the loaded bowl of tuna flakes on the grass, he licked his furry lips and went straight for it. Wasting no time, he lapped up the food greedily, munching everything in the bowl.

Shortly afterwards, a pain rose up in his gut.

Closing the gate for privacy, the woman at number thirty-seven knelt over the wheezing cat and watched it carefully. Its breathing was becoming shallower, its whining quieter, and its yellow eyes were beginning to close. It was all coming together nicely; all she had to do now was carry it out to the curb where she'd found poor Tabby, so that the oddball family could have their turn of finding their cat dead.

She wanted them to feel her pain, to get a taste of what she was experiencing. Maybe they'd know that she did it. Maybe they'd work out that it was a revenge attack, but so what? They were just as guilty as her, so what could they do?

Her only real concern was whether she'd put enough poison in the food to put their mangy pet into a permanent sleep.

Luna put a pair of slippers on her feet and walked out through the garden towards the communal car park. She'd just woken up and she needed her morning coffee. The jar she'd bought yesterday was nowhere to be seen, and she suspected that she might've left it in the car. As soon as she got outside, though, a black-and-white mound on the floor caught her eye.

'Bloody hell, it's still there!' she croaked, looking down at the cat's motionless, whiskered face. Running back into the house, she woke her husband. 'You know, I think we may have made a mistake digging that cat back up,' she said. 'It's still down there, right where we left it. It can't be a nice sight for the children who play out there.'

'Hhmm,' the husband groaned from under the covers. 'Look, the owner will find it soon enough.'

'But what if they don't?' Luna said, leaning over him. 'It's going to rot and decay. Somebody might catch something from it, or—'

'It's nothing to do with us, Luna! It's not our bloody cat!'

'Well, no, but...'

'But what?'

'But it is something to do with us, isn't it? Because we put it out there.'

After another painful groan, the husband rubbed his eyes and sat up. 'So, what do you want me to do? Bury the damned thing again?'

'I think it might be the best thing to do,' she said thoughtfully.

'Huh. Here we go again, then.' Chucking on a T-shirt and jogging bottoms, he grumpily walked out of the bedroom and descended the stairs.

'And be quick,' she called out after him. 'Try to do it before Clayton wakes up.'

Young Clayton was overcome with an acute sense of deja vu. Heading downstairs to make breakfast, he could hear his mother sobbing in despair. She was in a similar position as last time, on the sofa, peering out towards the back garden with tears running down her cheeks. Following her gaze, Clayton saw his father out on the grass with the shovel held high above his head.

The tip of the shovel was red.

'What's going on?' he asked.

His mother responded by jumping up to her feet and pushing him back out of the room.

'Go back upstairs, darling!' she cried. 'You shouldn't have to see this.'

'See what?' he said, looking out the back window to where his father was swinging the shovel about, using it like an axe.

'Just go back upstairs. You—'

'Oh, come on, Mum! I'm fourteen years old now! Just back off and tell me what's happening!'

She relented and then paced around the living room with her hands clasped over her face. 'That bloody cat was alive all along!' she wept. 'We buried the poor thing alive! And... And we almost did it again!'

'The cat was alive?' Clayton asked, looking outside as his father pummelled away at something on the grass. 'But...how?'

'Oh, who knows? We tried to bury it again, and the bloody thing started to move.'

'Why did you try to bury it again?'

'Oh, don't you start! Because we had to!'

Following an upward swing of his father's shovel, a fur-covered clump of flesh sailed through the air and then landed in an adjacent flowerbed. A second later, the shovel came back down again.

'You're... You're killing it,' Clayton whispered, observing what could only be described as a brutal massacre.

'Well, don't say it like that,' snapped his mum. 'We're putting it out of its misery.'

'Couldn't you have...'

'It wouldn't have lasted very long, Clayton. I have no idea what happened to it, but it couldn't even stand up. It was just rolling around, making horrible wheezing noises.'

'Do you still not know whose cat it is?'

'No,' replied his mother, stiffening up. 'And listen, don't you say a word to anyone about this, okay? Don't you go mouthing off to your little mates on the block. We could get into a serious row about this if the owners ever—'

'All right, don't worry,' said Clayton, backing off. Turning away from the window, he shook his head and went to make some cereal.

By the time he'd eaten breakfast and laced up his shoes, both of Clayton's parents were in the living room. The small grave outside had been filled and patted down for the second time, and there was a restored calm in the house.

After checking his pockets and picking up his bag, Clayton got ready to leave for school, but he lingered for a moment before going outside. 'See you later,' he said, nodding to both his parents.

His father gave him a silent nod, and his mother waved, wishing him a good day. With his hand resting on the back door handle, he prepared to walk outside, but a thought suddenly occurred to him. He turned, looking back towards the kitchen. Then, in a curious tone, he said, 'By the way, has anyone seen Jasper this morning?'

MUSINGS ON MORTALITY

Every life is a tainted clock
Ticking into decay
The hands, they only tick downwards
Going just one way

It's always there in the background
The harsh and ugly truth
A claw that grips and catches us
For that we need no proof

With no clear way of escaping
One can only postpone
All beings, so doomed from the start
Each one is on death row

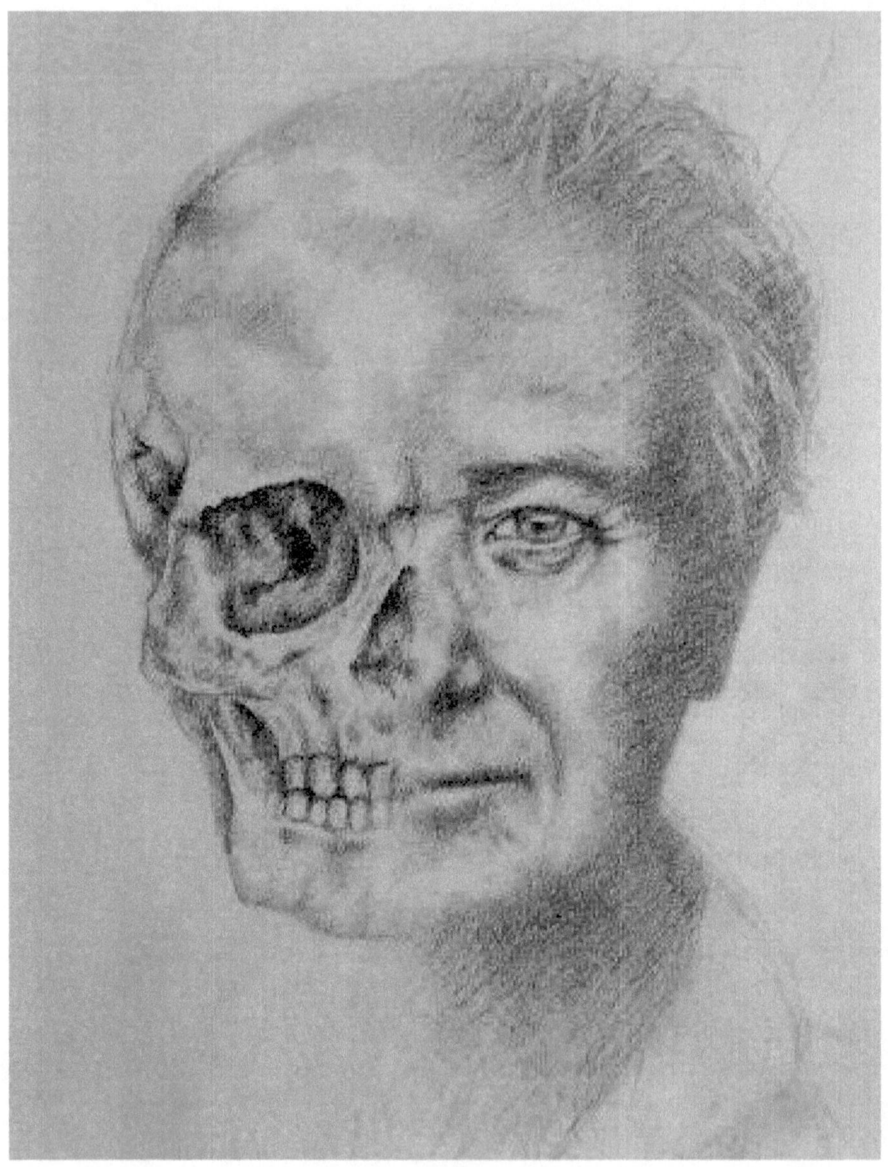

GUILT TRIP

They didn't really mean it
A stupid bit of fun
A silly prank one summer
All over with, and done

They had their fun and scarpered
Went their separate ways
The thing was all forgotten
Throughout their adult days

Who would have believed it?
So crazy, but so true
Their little misdemeanor
Did harm they can't undo

S hane sat in the mellow din of the coffee shop, sipping his hot drink as the morning traffic trickled by outside the window. There was work to be done, documents to be edited on his laptop in front of him, but it'd become a morning ritual for him to browse through the newspaper before beginning his daily chores.

The usual flurry of sensationalist headlines jumped out at him as he flicked through the pages: tax-avoiding politicians, celebrity love affairs, global warming threats, escalating wars, burglaries, murders, and a few crosswords and puzzles thrown in just to balance things out a bit.

'A load of old bloody tosh,' he muttered, scanning the columns and pictures.

There was one story, however, that caught his attention: a young woman from Clover Falls had been reported missing. *Clover Falls*. The name pulled his eyes towards the page like a magnet, drawing him in with its ghastly memories and associations. Clover Falls was a run-down town on the western outskirts of Mapharno City, a place that you avoided like the plague if you had any sense. Seeing the name of the place printed in the newspaper, Shane was amazed that it even existed still. He'd been there once or twice during his teenage years if he remembered correctly, just to explore the endless derelict buildings and warehouses that were scattered around there. *Shithole* was the word that sprang to mind as Shane sifted through his hazy memories of the town, distant memories that'd occurred during a misspent youth several decades ago.

A photo of a sweet-looking young lady with red hair was attached to the article, and Shane read through it with a morbid interest. According to the reporter, the girl was one of many people who'd gone missing in or around the old town in recent years, and a full-blown investigation was under way. Interviewed workers at a local hospital mentioned an incident a couple of days before the latest disappearance where a "drugged homeless man" was moved on by security after trying to steal medical supplies from one of their storage units, but the link between the two events was yet to be established. An adjoining sub article outlined a brief history of the crumbling town, along with stories from an assortment of citizens who claimed that pets had been going missing there for as long as they could remember.

'Some places never change,' grumbled Shane, folding the paper up and throwing it down on the table in disgust.

After gulping down the last mouthful of coffee from his steaming cup, he opened up one of the work documents on his laptop and got to work.

It was three a.m. and the chalky glow of the moon was shining in through Shane's bedroom window. He'd had a fairly busy day editing documents for his company, and he really should've been asleep, but he wasn't. He was usually a heavy sleeper, one of those people who dozed off minutes after his head touched the pillow, but tonight his mind was like a bulb with too many volts running through it. After jolting awake again, he sat up on his bed at a right angle, staring into a gloomy corner while beads of sweat dripped down his back and shoulders.

He knew.

That name, Clover Falls, had rattled him earlier on during the day, but at the time he didn't really know why. But now he did. Now he knew. He knew why the name of that rotten place had sent a shiver up his middle-aged spine. The nightmare he'd just woken up from had pieced the puzzle together, clicked the segments into place, and now the memory was there in his head as clear as a highly-polished pane of glass. *Clover Falls.* Damn right he'd been there before, he'd been there more than once during his troubled adolescence, but there was really only one single time that was relevant to his current state of panic.

Sitting there in the stuffy darkness, his naked body a clammy sack of damp meat, he relived the entire memory again in all its hilarious splendour. And it was hilarious, too. At least it was at the time...

It'd happened thirty years ago, three long decades. Shane was a seventeen-year-old tearaway who spent most of his days loitering around the local skatepark, getting into mischief with Vaughn, his partner in crime. They were referred to as the Deadly Duo by some, Double Trouble by others, and the other names that were thrown their way by disgruntled enemies were enough to make your ears bleed. They were skaters, they were drinkers, they were louts, they were thugs, and they were college dropouts with absolutely no direction and no future plans whatsoever other than to get wasted and have a laugh at somebody's expense.

On this particular night in question, the two of them were in the company of a local skater named Roland. They'd met Roland a week earlier on the mini ramp, drinking cheap cider and puffing away on roll-up cigarettes. Roland wasn't like most of the other boys at the park. He came from a well-to-do family in one of the nicer neighbourhoods, and unlike Shane and Vaughn he actually had plans in life. His weekend drinking and loitering at the skatepark was more of a temporary rebellious stage for young Roland, a passing fad before moving on to university to embark on a meaningful career.

Or at least it should've been.

Roland's father was a pathologist, a specialist in his field, and there was pressure on Roland to attend medical school and follow in his footsteps. This was rarely brought up by young Roland, unless he was really drunk or stoned, but most of the other kids knew about it.

On this boozy, mischievous night at the skate park, Shane had managed to get hold of a rare delicacy: a jar of LSD. This stuff was in liquid form, complete with a pipette. A local hoodlum who owed Shane money had given it to him as a form of payment, and he'd accepted it gratefully. Armed with this potent psychedelic, the plan for the evening's festivities had been simple: drink some beer, drop some acid, and then head over to Clover Falls to explore the derelict buildings.

There was always some kind of derelict building over at Clover Falls. Being the official toilet of Mapharno City, it was home to a wide array of crumbling factories, shops, and warehouses even back then. The latest addition to the rotting landscape, however, was a college. A few of the other kids had been over there a few days before, and tales of workshops full of tools, a gymnasium kitted out with sports equipment, and deserted classrooms and offices with discarded furniture ignited the adventurous spirits of all those around.

They weren't going there to steal anything; they were just going there to get high and explore the recently vacated facility in all its decadent glory.

And that's exactly what they did.

They all dropped the acid before they even arrived in Clover Falls, so by the time they got there they were pretty spaced out. They were giggling, wide-eyed, and seeing things through a lens of comical surrealism, walking along the empty streets like a group of aliens seeing planet Earth for the very first time. With the hallucinogen working its way around their bodies and distorting their vision, the empty college building looked like a cartoon funhouse as it appeared on the near horizon, its various sections and floors leaning and swaying in a wind that wasn't there.

All three of them were feeling the effects of the drug as they awkwardly stumbled across a messy field towards the college, but Roland was especially feeling them. Unlike Shane and Vaughn, he'd only gone as far as alcohol and cannabis in the past, and this strange trippy feeling taking over his senses was a completely new experience for him.

Entering the college was easy enough. The last group of teenage trespassers had busted the padlock on the main entrance doors, so they all walked in without any trouble. The electric hadn't been disconnected, so Shane flicked on every light switch that he passed, gulping down mouthfuls of beer as he led the way through the silent building. Graffiti already marked the walls and doors, but Vaughn added some more with a pen he brought along with him, with Shane climbing and hopping over the desks that'd been dragged out into the corridors. Roland was more apprehensive, tagging along a few metres behind them both while scanning the rooms through dilated pupils.

After around fifteen minutes or so of messing around, they sat down to smoke some cigarettes in what looked like an old carpentry workshop.

'I'm gettin' some mad visuals here,' laughed Shane, gazing around at the metal vices and files as they took on bizarre, mutated forms. 'Can you see that? I swear it's a robot or something.'

'It's a clamp,' chuckled Vaughn. 'You're just tripping. Mind you, can you see that sculpture over there? Is it a sculpture? Or is it a coat stand?'

'You idiot!' said Shane. 'That's a... Well, hang on. What actually is it?'

'I think it's a sculpture, but I'm not sure. Roland, what do you think that is? That wooden thing over in the corner?'

Shane and Vaughn both turned their heads towards Roland, then simultaneously cracked up with laughter as they saw that at some point he'd slid underneath the teacher's desk with his feet protruding out and pointing towards the ceiling. He was lying on his back under the desk, staring up at the underside of it, which was about ten inches away from his face.

'Roland, what—'

'There's so much room under here!' he cried, staring up at the bottom panel of the desk. 'You could... You could build a house under here!'

Shane and Vaughn were in stitches. Holding their stomachs, they rolled around in fits of laughter, howling and crying at how wasted their young friend was.

'Build a house?' Shane grinned. 'There's more room than that! You could easily build a block of flats or something, if you ask me!'

Another roar of laughter erupted between them, echoing slightly around the dusty workshop.

'He's wasted!' said Vaughn. 'Totally wasted!'

'It's okay, this'll sober him up a bit,' quipped Shane, leaning over towards Roland's beer can by the side of the desk.

'What are you doing?' whispered Vaughn, noticing that Shane had one hand dipped in the pocket of his coat.

Without answering, Shane pulled the jar of acid from his pocket and squeezed several large drops into the hole in the top of the beer can using the pipette, a hyena's grin spread across his face the whole time.

'No!' whispered Vaughn. 'He's out of it already! He can't have any more!'

'Calm down, Mr. Square. It's just a bit of acid.'

'You bastard,' giggled Vaughn. 'You total bastard.'

Shane pocketed the LSD and straightened himself up. 'Hey, Roland. Let's go and explore a bit more. And drink up! Your beer's gettin' flat!'

They both rose to their feet, taking in the moving walls and shadows all around them, waiting for Roland to get up from under the desk.

'Come on, Roland. Let's go for a walk. There are two other floors we haven't seen yet.'

'This desk is breathing,' said Roland. 'I'm sure it is.'

'Come on,' said Shane under his breath. 'Let's just leave him to it. He'll be all right.'

Vaughn took one last look at Roland's feet hanging out from under the desk, then shook his head and followed Shane out of the room.

'I wonder why this place went under,' said Shane, as the two of them wandered along the college's littered walkways.

'I don't know,' Vaughn answered dizzyingly. 'They sure had a lot of facilities.'

And it was true. Roaming around the old building, they'd seen textile workshops, a lecture hall, a gymnasium, and now they were confronted with a large drama theatre. To Shane and Vaughn's hallucinating brains, the place looked like a relic from another world. The big curtains flanking the stage resembled tall, cloaked guards watching them silently, and the array of dusty, frayed costumes lying about on the floor appeared to them as mutated slugs slithering this way and that.

'This place is crazy,' muttered Vaughn, the expression on his pale face one of wonder and fear.

'What's that up there?' asked Shane, gesturing towards the rear of the elevated stage.

'Only one way to find out,' replied Vaughn. 'Let's have a look.'

With awkward, drug-addled movements, they climbed up onto the big stage, stepped around the bundles of clothes, shoes, and costumes, then peeked behind one of the big curtains.

'Oh shit!' they cried in unison.

Behind the curtain, just off stage, a dozen faces peered up at them from the gloom. It was a terrifying sight, intensified by the tricks both of their minds were playing on them, but after a few seconds the reality of the situation became clear to them. They'd found a collection of mannequins piled up in a heap, with arms, legs, torsos, and heads all jutting out from the dust at random angles and configurations. The sight was so shocking to their intoxicated minds that even after they'd established the bodies weren't real, they still kept their distance from them and spoke tentatively.

'Props,' said Shane, clearing his throat.

'Huh?'

'They're props. They must've been used in plays and stuff.'

'Oh, yeah,' stammered Vaughn, peering down at the smooth, life-like features of the dolls.

'Hey, I've just had an idea.'

'What?'

'Let's tell Roland that they're medical examiners,' grinned Shane.

'Tell him what?'

'He's studying to become a pathologist. Let's arrange the mannequins to look like university professors or something, then tell him that they're here to assess his skills.'

'Get real, will you! He's not going to believe that.'

'Isn't he? He was talking about building a house under a bloody desk earlier. This'll be mild compared to that.'

'Yeah, but as soon as he walks in here he'll know that it's a drama theatre.'

'We'll move them to the lecture hall, then. Dress them up in some of these old costumes.'

Vaughn was now grinning like a Cheshire Cat. 'Come on, then. Let's do it.'

Giggling again like a couple of schoolgirls, they proceeded to carry the six-foot mannequins over to the lecture hall, along with a few bundles of clothes and costumes.

The plan was coming together.

'Hey, Roland, you'll never guess wh—'

Shane and Vaughn paused by the doorway of the carpentry workshop, stunned and stupefied by the sight that confronted them. Roland was standing upright, facing them, with one arm extended outwards as though he'd been paused mid-stride. The strange position he was in was unsettling enough, but it was his eyes that were truly alarming. They were like two pearly marbles bulging out of his face, displaying a look of insanity that bordered on being caricature.

An empty beer can lay on its side by his feet.

'What are you doing, Roland?' asked Shane.

'Don't come near me! Don't... Don't come near me!' he wailed through the side of his tight mouth. 'And don't touch me!'

'What's the matter?'

'I'm made of glass! I'm made of fucking glass! Don't touch me! If you touch me, I'll break!'

Noticing the empty beer can on the floor, Shane burst out laughing. Vaughn followed suit shortly afterwards, although his laughter was more hesitant. There was a trace of concern etched across his face, too, as though he could sense things were going a little too far.

'Come on, Roland!' shouted Shane. 'You can't mess around like this all night. You need to pull yourself together! It's time for your big exam!'

'Wh...What?' Roland squirmed, with the careful lip movements of a professional ventriloquist.

'It's your big chance! Have you forgotten? There's a group of medical examiners waiting for you upstairs! They're here to assess your operational skills!'

Poor Roland looked like he was going to burst from stress and panic. His teeth were chattering, his shoulders were shaking, and his legs were quivering like a dog preparing to defecate. 'Uhh! Uhn! No! No! Not now! I can't do it now! Not... Not like this!'

'You'll be fine,' smiled Shane, walking towards him with a sardonic grin. 'Don't worry, we believe in you. Don't we, Vaughn?'

Vaughn didn't say anything at first, but after a few moments he loosened up and went along with the ploy. 'Yes. We believe in you, Roland. We know you can do it.'

Roland was so off his face he didn't even look real. His pasty features were stuck in an open expression, gaping at the air like a sick fish, a cartoon character who'd seen a ghost. Shane took another step towards him.

'Don't touch me! I'm...I'm telling you, I'll shatter into a million pieces! I'll—'

'Come on now, Roland. You're being a bit silly. The most important exam of your whole entire life will begin in a few minutes, and you're rambling on about being made of glass. Snap out of it.'

After a little coaxing, Shane eventually managed to grab hold of Roland, and he shook him free of his psychosomatic glass illusion.

Vaughn silently watched on from the doorway, biting his nails.

'Do medical students even have to do this?' Vaughn whispered, walking a few paces behind Roland as they all made their way towards the lecture hall.

'I don't know, probably not. Mind you, there must be some kind of hands-on examination for a trainee pathologist at some point along the line. We're doing him a favour, really,' chuckled Shane. 'We're giving him a bit of practical experience.'

'Yeah,' said Vaughn, looking down towards his feet. 'Practical experience.'

The truth was that it didn't matter one iota how realistic this phony exam was, because Roland was so high he would've believed anything. He was way up there with the fairies, flying in ga-ga land, sailing along in another dimension. Every single drop of LSD that Shane had squeezed into his beer was now swimming through his bloodstream, swirling around his brain, and wreaking havoc with his perception of reality. It'd taken a full five minutes to get him properly moving again, and since then he'd claimed to be sinking in mud, melting into lava, growing extra fingers, and stuck in a giant cobweb that only he could see.

He was well and truly gone.

'Okay, this is it, Roland,' said Shane, putting on his sensible voice. 'The examiners are waiting in there,' he said, pointing to the closed doors of the lecture hall. 'But don't go in yet. You're scheduled for eleven thirty p.m., and the time now is eleven twenty-five p.m. If you go in too early, it won't look good.'

Roland lingered outside the big doors like a condemned man waiting to be led into a gas chamber. His bulbous eyes darted left and right continuously. 'I...I can't do this! I'm...I'm not ready! I'm not prepared!'

'Hey!' said Shane, pointing a finger at him sternly. 'What have I told you about this kind of talk? Me and Vaughn have complete faith in you. Don't let us down by having silly little doubts about yourself.' Then, after waiting a moment, he added, 'And what will your father say if you mess this up? Have you thought about that?'

Roland looked so distraught that Vaughn had to turn and walk away.

'Anyway,' said Shane, noticing Vaughn's departure, 'we'll leave you to it. Good luck! You can tell us all about it later on.'

And just like that, Roland was left standing outside the doors of the lecture hall on his own, searching his spangled brain for the medical procedures and technicalities that he knew. Meanwhile, Shane and Vaughn sneaked around a corner towards a rear door that led into the lecture hall from the back. They then quietly entered the large room and sat down between two wigged, clothed mannequins in the back row of seats.

The lecture hall was as silent as a tomb, with the dozen or so "examiners" rigidly perched on their seats, waiting for their student to enter the room. The lectern had been taken away and replaced with a table, and upon the table lay the cadaver: a naked female mannequin with starchy red hair and pinky-red lips. An assortment of kitchen knives from the canteen were carefully positioned around her, complete with a tattered pair of rubber gloves.

Despite having set the whole thing up, Shane and Vaughn felt very tense and unsettled as they sat there observing the fruits of their labour. It felt a little bit too real, a little bit too elaborate, and there was a sense that the joke had morphed into something else. In fact, Vaughn actually leaned over towards Shane to voice his concerns and tell him that things had gotten out of hand, but just as he opened his mouth to speak, the big entrance doors began to creak open.

———

'I can't take this anymore,' said Vaughn. 'I'm going.'

The two of them had been sitting in an awkward, guilty silence for what seemed like an hour, watching their stupid prank unfold into a cruel nightmare. Roland was still up there on the stage, speaking to the rows of examiners with exaggerated courtesy and politeness as he hacked away at the plastic mannequin. He was shaking like a leaf, his fingers trembling as he nervously guided the sea of onlookers through his procedure.

It was never supposed to go this far. They'd expected a few minutes of silly fun, followed by a transgression into some other joke or adventure in another section of the building. But there was nothing funny about what they were seeing. They were witnessing a traumatic breakdown in slow motion, a tragic loss of dignity, a disintegration of a young man's soul.

And he was still as high as a kite.

Shane and Vaughn were beginning to come down from their trips a little bit, sobriety returning to them as the night wore on, but young Roland was still lost in a chemical haze. His irises were completely consumed by his ever-growing pupils, his jaw was permanently clenched, and his entire being jittered and trembled with a malignant otherworldliness. Watching young Roland relentlessly skittering about on the platform with his inhuman eyes focused on the blades, a terrifying suspicion dawned on both Shane and Vaughn, but it was too hideous for either of them to mention.

Responding to Vaughn's comment, Shane said, 'Yeah, let's go. This is getting too weird.'

As slowly and discreetly as possible, they both rose from their seats and crept out of the rear door of the lecture hall, leaving Roland to his incessant cutting, slicing, and dissecting of the red-haired female on the table. Within minutes they were hurling themselves down the staircase towards the ground floor and charging out of the building into the cold night air.

Retreating across the wispy field on which the college stood, they turned their heads and gazed up at the lecture hall window from a distance. A series of elongated shadows danced and bobbed across the visible sections of wall and ceiling as the sole occupant tirelessly entertained his inanimate crowd, trapped all alone in a seamless bubble of fear and delusion.

Over thirty years had passed since that awful night, and now, sitting in the gloom of his bedroom in the early hours of the morning, Shane remembered it all in vivid detail. Young Roland's drugged face rose up into his consciousness every time he thought about the newspaper article, the details of the case too coincidental to ignore. Had he, in a moment of childish mischief three decades ago, created a killer? The article mentioned nothing of murder, but his intuition was filling in the gaps.

He never did get back to sleep that night, nor did he sleep properly for the next few weeks. The press continued to report missing people in and around the western outskirts of Mapharno City, and every time Shane read through the details of the cases he became more and more convinced that he knew who the culprit was.

But it couldn't be true, it just couldn't be. It was too ridiculous to even contemplate. Three long decades had come and gone, the world was a different place, and Shane was now a middle-aged man with a balding head and a bloated gut. The prank had occurred in the distant past, during the pre-mobile phone and pre-internet era, a time when there were only a handful of TV stations to choose from. Could young Roland still be... The very thought chilled Shane to the bone, but he couldn't shake it off.

What should he do? Go to the police? Maybe. But his story was just too tenuous to share with anyone, especially the boys in blue. Contacting Vaughn was also out of the question, because Shane had no idea where he lived or whether he was even still alive. Contact between the two of them had fizzled out not long after the night in Clover Falls, and he had no real way of tracking him down.

How Shane dearly hoped that he was wrong. Pacing around his apartment week after week as more and more victims went missing, there was nothing that would've satisfied him more than a discovery that the perpetrator of the crimes was someone else entirely, proving his theory to be nothing other than a paranoid delusion.

But would that discovery ever come?

It had to be done. For the sake of his mental health, it had to be done. If he ever wanted to get a decent night's sleep again, it had to be done.

He had to visit Clover Falls.

The purpose of the trip was to put his mind at rest. He'd go there, find the old college building—if it even still existed—discover it was empty, then return home with a clear conscience, ready to get on with the rest of his life and put these stupid thoughts behind him.

That was the plan.

Finding the old town was trickier than he thought it'd be. Everything looked so different. A train took him to the outskirts of the city, but there were no functional stations within a five-mile radius of Clover Falls. After getting off the train, he walked through a series of rough neighbourhoods, with slack-jawed simpletons and poverty-stricken children watching him from doorsteps, then crossed a number of overgrown fields littered with burnt tyres and plastic.

Clover Falls was little more than a sparsely populated rubbish tip, but to Shane's surprise some of the old buildings were still visible on the near horizon, including the college. The very sight of the old college building, now almost ancient in its antiquity, was like a cold hand gripping Shane's heart, its mouldy exterior injecting him with ice.

A visible pathway extended across the field to the college's entrance.

This pathway was mainly visible due to the setting sun that shone from the west, throwing a warm hazy light over the trampled grass. Following the trail, Shane took his chances with the main entrance doors. They were filthy and covered in grime, but they opened up with a sturdy push.

After a quick look around, he stepped inside.

The lower floor of the building instantly brought it all back, flashbacks of his younger self jumping over desks and goofing around. The layout of the place was the same, but dust and rubble coated everything, and a stagnant, stale musk hung in the air.

Gravitating towards the first floor, he found himself outside a large room that he believed to be the carpentry workshop. Putting his hand on the door handle, he closed his eyes for a second and hoped that the old room was empty. He hoped to see nothing but splintered wooden desks and rusty vices, the innocent remnants of a class full of aspiring apprentices.

His hope was in vain.

As soon as the door opened, a gassy stench hit his nostrils like a jackhammer, a putrid scent that made him gag and double over. And then, once his eyes had stopped watering, he saw the carnage laid out before him. The rows of carpentry worktops were covered in fleshy mounds piled on top of each other, all buzzing with flies and maggots. An assortment of anatomical parts littered the desks and tabletops: calves, hands, forearms, feet, and even heads. Blood-stained saws sat amongst the decaying clumps of tissue and bone, their serrated edges matted with powdered bone fragments and pus. Cracked skulls with mouldy skin peeling from them were wedged in the steel vices, and buckets of sloppy organs and intestines lined the walls.

Shane had experienced several nightmares over the last few weeks, but none of them were as gruesome as the scene that confronted him right now.

A noise sounded off from somewhere overhead.

It was a muffled sound, a bit like a vibration or a voice. Someone was talking, or... *No, it can't be!* thought Shane.

The voice got progressively louder as he climbed the grimy stairs, the words vibrating around the flaking walls and peeling handrails. Upstairs, the lecture hall doors appeared in the distance like an entrance to hell. He was drawn towards them like a moth towards a flame, his footsteps carrying him towards the horror that he knew was waiting for him.

The doors were ajar, and he peered inside.

The lecture hall seats were all occupied, smiling faces beaming up towards the stage. The figures sat with their stiff arms folded on their laps and wild mops of hair springing out from their plastic scalps. Dust motes covered the shoulder pads of their retro outfits, cobwebs stretched across the creases of their ears, and their shiny features were cracked and dulled by time. Shane recognised them all, their joyous, comical expressions appearing to him as long-lost acquaintances.

One face he didn't recognise, however, was the one up on the stage.

It was only after a certain amount of gaping and squinting that Shane was able to confirm to himself that it was Roland up there.

He had matted grey hair that clung to his head in greasy knots, a hunched back resulting from the countless hours bent over the examination table, and lines and wrinkles on his skin that were deeper than a seabed. The voice that rang out from his chattering mouth sounded like an untuned, damaged wind instrument, and then...

And then there was his stare.

From a short distance away, Roland's eyes looked like holes in the ground. Exhausted and spent through years of chemical stupor and insomnia, his entire countenance had a terminal look to it. There was a rot to his gaze, his wide pupils sitting over a network of red scraggly veins, psychosis oozing from every watery corner. The tortured stare of a zoo animal locked in a cage and forgotten about for three decades would've been something for him to aspire to, such was the decay of his stare.

But what concentration and focus!

Hunched over the table in front of him, he delicately peeled away layer after layer of skin and tissue from the slab of meat, cutting and slicing deftly as the dust-covered examiners smiled and watched from their crumbling seats. *Slab of meat.* That's what it looked like at first glance, anyway. It was only when he noticed the locks of red hair falling down the sides of the table that Shane consciously realised who—or what—was on it.

Oh, Roland! What have you done? Now that the shock and terror of it all was beginning to subside, a sense of intense tragedy and despair washed over Shane as he secretly watched from the doorway. The blood, the mess, the horror, it was all...his fault. *What have you done?* That was not the correct question, he decided. The correct question was: *What have I done?* It was all his doing, all of it. He was to blame. Him and his stupid prank.

'Me,' he whispered through his own quivering lips. 'It's all because of me.'

Staggering back from the doors of the lecture hall, he gulped a few lungfuls of air and tried to get his wits about him. A tremendous weight was pressing down upon him, the weight of guilt and responsibility. He wanted to leave, to run away and once again forget that any of it had ever happened, but he was tethered to the horrific affair by his guilt and culpability.

It took a while for Shane to work out what he needed to do, but eventually the idea came to him like a crystalline epiphany, a ray of light that promised to make amends.

The shaky, manic voice that rattled through the lecture hall was punctuated by sickly wet cutting sounds as more and more sections of the cadaver were dissected. A stuttered commentary was given to the examiners as each organ and piece of muscle was lifted away, a brief explanation for each slice and cut. The examiners, for their part, were watching the student's performance in silence, giving off an air of detached professionalism. The student had no idea how long he'd been up there for. Minutes blended into minutes, hours blended into hours, and his mind as usual was a continuous fog of shapes and colours. The examiners never spoke, the examiners never moved, but he knew that they always watched him intensely.

Then something changed.

About two rows down, there was some movement. One of the examiners cleared his throat, then rose slowly from his seat. Raising a hand in the air, he halted the student's presentation.

'That's enough, young man. That'll be all. Well done. You've passed.'

Frozen in motion, the student gazed out towards the lines of medical examiners, his jaw hanging loose like a slack door hinge. His red, bulbous eyes surveyed the room with the controlled intensity of a tightrope walker tip-toeing on piano wire, then, with his pained, piercing voice, he said, 'Okay, sir. Thank you very much,' before placing a dripping kidney back down inside the gaping hole in the corpse's stomach and walking gingerly out of the room.

A fleet of police cars and a sizeable crowd of curious locals and press reporters were gathered outside the cordon of the college grounds, and an air of excitement resonated amongst everyone. After the local constabulary received a call from a man claiming to be behind the spate of disappearances in the area, word soon spread and details were passed around. They all watched on as armed officers charged across the field towards the crumbling building, ready to make their arrest.

And they didn't have to wait very long for them to return. Within five minutes a cluster of people could be seen emerging from the old college, pushing a cuffed man in front of them.

'We got him,' they announced as they drew nearer. 'We've got our man.'

'Stand back, please!' shouted another officer, who was in charge of controlling the crowd. 'Stand back and make way!'

Most of the locals obeyed the order, but the press reporters moved closer to the action like hungry flies buzzing around shit.

'What's his name?' called one of them, holding a microphone.

'Are any of the victims still alive?' yelled another, with a chunky camera in his hands.

Once the detainee was safely secured in the back of one of the cars, the officer in charge of crowd control tucked a loose part of her shirt back in, straightened her belt, then addressed the assemblage of people.

'We're not in a position to disclose any information at this point, but please rest assured there'll be an official announcement at some point over the next couple of days.'

'How many victims are in there?' asked a reporter.

'I really can't say right now. Sorry.'

'How long has...*he* been in there for?' asked a local, leaning over a cameraman's shoulder.

'Please, all of your questions will be answered in due course,' replied the officer. 'The forensics examiners need to go in there and check the scene for—'

'The examiners are already in there,' came a jumpy voice from the crowd.

The officer, momentarily stumped and confused after being interrupted by such a random comment, scanned the bustling crowd to try and locate the person who'd said it. But there were too many people there by this point, too many jostling heads, and she gave up after a few seconds. Clearing her throat and gathering her thoughts, she carefully continued: 'The... The examiners are not here yet. But they will arrive shortly, and so we need you all to move on and clear the area for them. Please return to your homes. Thank you.'

The crowd dispersed, people breaking up and going off in their own directions. The reporters got back in their cars and sped off with their photos and recordings, the locals returned to their doorsteps and living rooms, and a couple of the police cars drove back towards the local station.

A little further out, however, along the main avenue that led to the district hospital, a lone figure walked proudly off into the sunset. A wide, satisfied grin lit up his twisted face, illuminating his aged features. All of his hard work had paid off. He'd done it.

He'd passed the assessment.

THE SOUL DESTROYER

He ventured into the tropics, to study a parasite
And while he was out in the jungle, he had an awful fright
Whatever it was that he saw, it certainly took its toll
It sucked away his will to live, and then it destroyed his soul

The car pulled up at the curb in the middle of the sleepy, residential street, then came to a gentle stop. On each side of the road, amid the neat rows of trees trailing off into the distance in either direction, brown semi-detached houses sat behind their well-tended gardens and tidy driveways. When the driver's door opened a stout, suited man climbed out, his neatly-combed head turning left and right as he looked for a door number. Once he found what he was looking for, he straightened his tie and proceeded to walk up one of the gravel driveways, his polished shoes crunching the small stones as he went.

Inspector Griffin was the Chief Inspector at HCQ, the organisation responsible for investigating hospitals and mental institutions across the UK. His visit to this leafy, suburban street was regarding an ongoing investigation at Bryson Psychiatric Hospital, a secure facility for the mentally ill situated out in the Kentish countryside. It'd been a very bad few months for the hospital, what with an unusually large amount of staff members either leaving or being struck off sick. A wave of resignations and sicknesses of this size and magnitude was virtually unheard of, and so it soon prompted an investigation.

The address he'd just arrived at belonged to a nurse who was currently on sick leave from Bryson Hospital due to severe stress and anxiety, and according to the latest reports, her condition wasn't getting any better. Her situation was beginning to become a very common one for nurses working at this particular facility. Just a few days ago, Griffin had visited the home of another nurse who'd swallowed a bottle of painkillers in an attempt to end her own life. She'd been in a catatonic state when he'd arrived, her family attending to her needs and feeding her, and so his efforts to get some useful information from her had been futile. He'd sat there in that house for over an hour, listening to the woman's distraught husband describe her strange behaviour while she herself sat in the corner staring out of the window, her glazed, unblinking eyes filled with a haunted look that Griffin could still see now in his mind's eye. He'd listened as her relatives described in detail the wails and cries that came out of her room at night, as well as informing him that they now had to keep all sharp objects and harmful medicines hidden from her at all times. After making some notes and thanking the family for their time, he'd left the house with a deep-set belief that the nurse was never going to return to work again.

Despite the peculiar nature of this recent spate of absences and resignations, its actual cause wasn't a complete mystery. Griffin knew the basic reason why the staff members were leaving and falling ill, but at the same time he just couldn't quite believe it. Several senior nurses and lower-level managers were being very bold and forthright about their opinions and theories, but neither Griffin nor his seniors at HCQ could take them seriously. Most of them were claiming that employees were leaving due to a new patient who'd been admitted to the hospital five months ago and that a brief look into his eyes was all it took for one to lose one's mind.

Griffin found all of this ridiculous, but at the same time he had to acknowledge that this new patient was indeed a unique case. The man was a biologist, specialising in parasitology, with a distinguished career; he was Cambridge educated, had several scientific articles in well-respected journals published under his name, a list of degrees and accolades as long as his arm, and a legacy within the scientific community that even Charles Darwin or Isaac Newton would have been proud of. Griffin doubted that any mental institution in the land had ever had anyone of such status under their roof, and his sectioning was indeed an enigma.

The biologist, known to all as Professor Avery, was sectioned under the mental health act following a state-funded work expedition in the tropics of South America. Griffin had personally gone through his hospital file with a fine-tooth comb, reading everything he could about him. Details of the work expedition were fortunately available for him to read, and he'd scoured them obsessively, trying to gain some kind of clue as to what had happened. According to the files, Professor Avery had travelled to a jungle region of Panama to study a certain type of parasitic nematode. A small team of coworkers and biology students had flown out there with him to assist him in the process of recording data, but Avery had been the main figurehead of the project.

It became apparent after reading the file that the professor had seen something out there that had caused him to lose his mind, making him lose his grip on reality. Officers from a tiny local constabulary out in a Central American village were called when locals reported a foreign man behaving erratically and attacking several residents, and additional charges were put forward after the professor made violent advances towards officers in the station. Photographs of bite marks on one officer's arm were attached to the report for Griffin to see, as was the bruising to one officer's face who had to open Avery's cell door when he attempted to hang himself with his own belt. UK officials had been called in to assist with Avery's deportation, and several more violent outbursts had been recorded during the process.

Since his arrival at Bryson Hospital, however, Avery had slipped into a prolonged bout of silence and withdrawal, with not one single word being heard from him during the five months of his incarceration. He refused to eat, drink, or communicate with anyone, but despite the adoption of this antisocial behaviour there had been no reports of abusive or threatening behaviour of any kind, no cases of injuries sustained to any of the nurses who tended to him. On paper the professor was a harmless patient, a physical threat to no one, but his presence within the hospital was still dangerous somehow. Trauma and torment seemed to ooze from his every pore, and those who had gazed into his deep-set, wizened eyes claimed to have felt his pain on a kind of telepathic level. And as if this wasn't strange enough, these claims went even further still. One nurse in particular, the second one to resign after the professor's arrival, claimed to have seen a mental image after making eye contact with him, as though some kind of grainy picture had been transferred across to her through his stare.

Indeed, it was this atmosphere that Avery had created within the facility that was supposedly responsible for the numerous resignations and absences, this profound effect that he had on those in his close vicinity. Griffin had not yet been granted permission to see Professor Avery in person due to this risk of health, but apparently, according to certain rumours, his face was now permanently covered up to prevent any more incidents of this nature. Descriptions of some kind of bag had been spoken of unofficially, a kind of thin veil secured around his head and neck to protect nurses from his dangerous stare. In addition to this, the professor was on constant suicide watch, the small metal hatch on his cell door left open to allow the wardens a clear view of his movements and actions.

Putting aside the brief, violent outbursts in Central America surrounding his arrest, Professor Avery didn't seem to want to do anyone any harm; his suicidal tendencies were simply contagious to those around him whether he wanted them to be or not, and it was for this reason that he was considered to be a very dangerous man.

Griffin approached the front door of the suburban house, then rang the bell. After a few moments, a blurred figure appeared behind the stained glass, then a polite, unassuming man opened the door and welcomed him in.

'She's upstairs,' said the man, who was obviously the nurse's husband. 'Do you want to go up and see her?'

'Yes, please,' said Griffin before following him up a dim, carpeted staircase.

'I'm not sure how much you'll be able to get out of her. She's been very quiet today.'

'What has she told you?' whispered Griffin, lowering his voice as the two of them reached the upper landing.

'Very little. She's hardly spoken to me at all since it all happened. In fact, she speaks more in her sleep than she does during her waking hours.' The man paused for a second, rubbing the bags under his eyes. 'There are noises in the early hours of the morning: screams, yells, swearing. She sleeps in the spare room now. It's... It's better that way.'

'She has nightmares?'

'Every night.'

'Do you know what they're about?'

'Every time I try to speak to her, she switches off.'

Griffin noticed a faint quiver in his voice, a light trembling, and decided not to press him any further. The distress of it all was evident on his face, the screams and sleepless nights had etched lines around his brow and temple.

'Where's the...spare room?'

'It's over there,' he said, nodding his head towards the end of the hallway.

'Thank you.'

The woman's husband forced a smile, then skulked back towards the staircase. As soon as he was out of sight, Griffin put his ear to the bedroom door and listened closely for any sounds. Hearing none, he then knocked on it a couple of times. The room sounded echoey from the other side, his knocks ringing through the air for longer than they should have. Out of politeness and courtesy he waited a long time for a reply, but hearing none, he eventually turned the handle and let himself in.

The room was bare and empty, with just a single bed and a chair in the corner. The curtains were half-drawn, casting a faint grey light over everything, and the air was still. A woman was lying on the bed, her head propped up with two pillows and her body covered with a thin bedsheet. She didn't move or stir when Griffin entered the room, nor was there any noticeable change in her blank expression. He almost felt alone as he walked in and stood by the end of the bed, like he was in a room with a mannequin or a wax-work model in a museum. Eventually, after several polite attempts to communicate with her, he quietly sat himself down on the chair in the corner, watching her the whole time.

Her face was so pale that it blended and merged with the pillow, her pinky-red bloodshot eyes the only thing with any real colour to them. She was floating somewhere between consciousness and unconsciousness, awake and not awake, lost in her own lonely realm. In fact, she was so utterly unresponsive and unmoved to Griffin's presence that he wondered, for a brief second, whether she might have passed away without her husband knowing. This suspicion didn't last too long, however, because upon close inspection he could see that a slight tremor ran through her body at regular intervals, a kind of shudder that shook her torso and made the bed frame creak. It was so minute and subtle that it could've easily been missed, but now that he was close to her he could see it.

'What happened to you? What made you ill?' he whispered into her ear.

There was no response to these words, no flicker or flinch in her countenance.

'Did Professor Avery do this to you?'

The faint creaking of the bed frame was still the only sound in the room, but even so, Griffin detected some kind of shift after he'd mentioned the professor's name, some alteration deep within her.

'Did you…interact with him in any way?'

Now there was noticeable movement, so noticeable, in fact, that it made Griffin jump. The nurse's breathing became heavier and audible, her chest rising and falling under the sweaty sheets. He was sure that she could hear him now, sure that he wasn't just talking to himself. It was the mention of the professor's name that had initially gotten through to her, so he deliberately mentioned it again in an effort to open her up some more.

'Did you…look at Professor Avery?'

A pinprick of light glistened from somewhere in the pale folds of her face, and Griffin realised, with tense surprise, that it was a tear in the corner of her eye. The grey light seeping in through the curtains was just bright enough to reflect against it, exposing some inner emotion the nurse was evidently experiencing. She was about to crack, and Griffin moved in closer.

'Speak to me. Nobody can help you unless you speak to them.'

Her thin lips began to tremble and blubber, and with a weak cry she said, 'There... There's no helping this.'

'There's no helping what?'

Her face was screwed up in pain now, and she turned her head towards the window.

'What did he do to you?'

'He didn't... He didn't do anything,' she sobbed. 'He just...made me see.'

'See what?'

The tears were rolling down her cheeks now, and she brought one of her hands up from under the covers to wipe them. As she did so, a pungent odour wafted out across the room, hitting home the fact that she hadn't washed or left the bed in days. Her torment was detectable in every aspect of her being; when she spoke, it was like she was speaking from the depths of a deep cave within her mind, a cave that she'd carved out for herself to escape whatever was haunting her.

'I... I won't talk about it! I won't! It's... It's just too horrible!'

'How did he make you see? How did he do it?'

The tears and chokes were coming on strong now, too strong for the woman to answer coherently, but Griffin wasn't going to give up.

'Did you look into his eyes?'

In between the heaving sobs and shudders, the nurse managed to nod her head in confirmation.

'And then what? What happened when you looked into his eyes?'

'They... They were just so full of...misery. The... The way he looked at me...sucking me into those two black pits!'

'And what did you see? Tell me what you saw!'

The nurse was now hysterical. Her sobs had turned into high-pitched wails and cries, echoing around the bare, empty room and shaking the walls. The door burst open unexpectedly, and the woman's husband leaned in with a stern look about him.

'I think that's enough,' he said. 'She's not well enough for this.'

With the nurse shaking and hollering next to him as she was, Griffin couldn't protest. He rose from the small chair and made his way out, leaving the husband to tend to her. Outside, standing by his car next to the road, he could still hear the woman's screams.

Visiting the two nurses had had an unsettling effect on Griffin. He'd still been very sceptical after seeing the first one, despite her chronic state, but after seeing both of them and witnessing their compounded trauma and distress firsthand, he was left with no choice but to at least consider the far-fetched theory that the professor was somehow contaminating people with his thoughts. Whether there was a supernatural element to any of it, he couldn't be sure, but there was certainly no denying the fact that the two employees had seen something whilst in his presence—something that'd destroyed their souls and made them lose the will to live.

He knew what had to be done next. It was an inevitable, unavoidable task that simply had to be endured if he was to get to the bottom of this case and put it to bed: he was going to have to visit the hospital and meet Professor Avery in person. The senior staff at Bryson Hospital had not been allowing any visits to the professor for quite some time now, not even to HCQ inspectors, but with enough persistence on Griffin's part, combined with a firm letter from the Chief Executive, he knew that they would have to eventually give in. Sitting in his home study, in front of his thick wooden desk piled high with folders, Griffin resolved to get this process in motion today. First, though, before he could even begin to prepare himself for the daunting, intimidating prospect of meeting Professor Avery in the flesh, he wanted to go through his file one more time.

He had a decent amount of information at his disposal, a large stack of papers about an inch thick. The sequence of events that'd happened during the professor's expedition were already known to him, almost committed to memory, in fact, but Griffin wanted to learn a bit more about the actual parasite that Avery was studying at the time. Flicking through the assortment of papers, he found the typed-up notes that the professor had made prior to, and during, his expedition.

He read slowly and carefully, taking his time, eager to learn more about this bizarre creature.

Classification: Parasitic nematode/roundworm.

Habitat: Tropical forests of Central America/South America.

Known hosts: Cephalotes Atratus Ant. Bananaquit bird. Tryant flycatcher bird.

Life cycle: The host ant, Cephalotes Atratus, gets infected by the nematode after eating the infected fecal matter of either the Bananaquit bird or the Tryant flycatcher bird. Once infected, the ant falls prey to the parasite, displaying a sluggishness and change in behaviour. As well as this, the ant will also take on a physical change in appearance. It's abdomen (usually black in colour) will swell up in size (due to being filled with nematode eggs) and take on a bright shade of red, then, after this transformation of its body is complete, the ant will feel compelled to climb up a long blade of grass in the near vicinity and stick its red, swollen abdomen up in the air. To passing birds (namely the Bananaquit and Tyrant) the ant's swollen abdomen will strongly resemble a ripe berry, tempting the bird to swoop down and consume it. Once the bird has been tricked into eating this infected section of the ant's body, the eggs will pass through its body and get excreted out, therefore spreading the eggs out into further ant colonies.

Griffin slapped the papers back down on his desk, then ran a hand through his hair. He was at a loss at what to make of this. This parasite, or nematode, or whatever it was, sounded vile, but he still couldn't imagine how or why someone would go insane after seeing it. The professor had completely lost it out there in the Central American tropics, running around attacking people like a wild man, and although the details of this ant-infecting parasite were ghastly and horrid, they just couldn't account for such dramatic behaviour.

Pulling out his phone, he scrolled down until he found the Chief Executive's number. He knew that he would have to get the professor to open up to him if he was to solve this riddle, but before that could happen the Chief Executive would have to persuade Bryson Hospital to allow a visit.

The psychiatric facility had a cold, austere look to it, the iron gates and brown brickwork completely unwelcoming and featureless. There was a still, silent feel to the air, and as Griffin parked his car he looked up at the rows of reinforced glass windows, wondering whether the atmosphere was any better inside. The receptionist told him to sit down and wait for a senior nurse who'd escort him through the building, and he did so without complaint.

The senior nurse was a petite woman with mousy hair and a familiar-sounding voice. Griffin had never met her before but was sure that he'd spoken to her over the phone at some point. She was accompanied by a heavyset man who wore a similar white uniform to hers, and after a brief exchange the three of them swiped through a set of security doors and made their way down towards the maximum-security wing.

'The professor's been transferred to maximum security following the recent problems,' said the nurse as they walked down a sterile-looking white corridor with cells on either side. 'He's not displayed any violent behaviour, but... Well, he's proven himself to be a threat in his own way.'

'So I've heard,' replied Griffin.

'We've also taken the precaution of covering up his face. This may seem a little unnecessary, but we think it's a sensible move.'

'So it's true then?'

'I'm sorry?'

'It's true that you're covering up his face?'

'Inspector Griffin, we had to do something. Several staff members have fallen ill after looking—'

'I know, I know,' said Griffin, interjecting her in a polite way so she didn't have to go through all of the grizzly details, 'I just wasn't sure whether it was true or not. There's no mention of it in the report.'

'It's a spit hood,' she said candidly. 'It's a thin mesh spit hood. It doesn't cause him any discomfort of any kind, other than maybe restricting his vision a little bit.'

'Has he been cooperative with this decision?'

'Yes, he certainly has. He hasn't protested about anything since he's been here.'

Griffin nodded thoughtfully. 'And he's still not speaking to anyone?'

'No. You don't get a single word out of him all day. He's been here for five months now, and I don't even know what he sounds like.'

'So have people tried speaking to him?'

'We did when he first arrived, but...' The woman's voice trailed off for a second. '...but not anymore.'

They walked the rest of the way in silence, an uneasiness lingering between them as they descended further down into the building.

It took about five minutes to reach the professor's cell. Griffin knew that he'd arrived before being told, the open hatch on the metal door being the main giveaway. There were two other beefy-looking male nurses outside the cell, one crouching down to look through the hatch. The men had obviously been informed of Griffin's visit, because they prepared themselves to open the door without being told, one fumbling for a key on his hip, the other searching for a set of restraints in his pocket. Once everything was in place and the key was being inserted into the lock, the senior nurse turned towards Griffin with a serious look in her eye.

'Don't get too close to him. As I said, he's not known to be violent, but you've seen the damage he can do to people.'

'Yes,' said Griffin, trying his best to cover up his shaking hands.

Sensing his nervousness, she then added, 'We'll be right here the whole time,' before dutifully giving a nod to the big nurse with the key.

The lock snapped open, the door opened wide, and Griffin, sweating under his shirt collar, took a few deep breaths and then entered.

The cell was at a contrast to the corridor outside. It was dim and stale, with just a single overhead bulb for light. A dark mound sat slumped in the corner, shrouded in shadow, and Griffin stood there for a few long moments watching it, paralysed with tension and fear. The professor looked thin and frail under the hospital slacks, his delicate frame barely visible under the baggy folds. His head was no different, of course, the mesh hood concealing everything from the neck up. It was unclear whether the professor actually knew he was there or not, as there'd been no movement from him at all. The mesh spit hood sat over his head like a starched pillowcase, giving absolutely nothing away, its stiff creases concealing its contents.

The silence in the cell was so all-encompassing, so total and complete, that it felt wrong for Griffin to break it, but he had to start somewhere.

'Professor Avery?' he said, squinting into the shadows.

The words came out as a croaky whisper, and he had to clear his throat before he went on.

'I'm Inspector Griffin, Chief Inspector at HCQ. May I speak to you?'

He received nothing by way of reply. Complete silence resumed, broken only by the faint sound of distant shouting from somewhere down the corridor outside.

'Do you mind if I sit down?'

There was no response, but at the same time there was no objection, either, so he sat down and leaned back against the opposite wall. There was still a safe distance of about seven feet between them, but Griffin was now close enough to see the professor more clearly, the shapes and contours of his form coming into focus. The thin veil of the hood did its job of hiding the professor's face, but rather worryingly, it didn't obscure it completely. Bony, chiselled features were discernible through its thin material, and Griffin had to make a constant conscientious effort not to stare at them for too long. The dim outlines and crevices enshrouded within the hood were so starved and gaunt in their appearance that they vaguely resembled a skull rather than a living human head, the bridge of the nose and cheekbones protruding through pale skin.

'Will you talk to me, Professor?'

Again, there was not as much as a flicker of response.

'What happened to you, Professor? What did you see out in the tropics?'

It was hard to believe that this introverted, crumpled figure opposite him was the same man that Griffin had read about. The numerous mentions of exemplary conduct rose up to the forefront of his mind, graduation photographs accompanied by pages of accolades, acclaimed published scientific articles, too many degree certificates to count, and it all came from this mute, incarcerated mess sitting before him, this absolute wreck of a human being. His fear was rapidly turning into sympathy the longer he sat there opposite Avery, but at the same time, the memory of the two sick nurses he'd seen forced him to keep his guard up.

'I want to understand what happened to you. I'm not here to judge you on anything. Why don't you talk to me?'

Another bout of silence tested Griffin's patience even further, but he wasn't done yet.

'I've read a lot about your career, Professor. There are many people out there who have much praise for you.'

For a split second, Griffin thought he saw movement in the professor's hands, a slight tremble running all the way down to the fingernails that'd been chewed to stumps. It could've just been a trick of the light, however, because nothing else followed it. Five minutes passed by, then ten, with Griffin trying his hardest to break through the thick wall that the professor had built around himself, but it was to no avail. Reaching his limit of patience and perseverance, he made a few loose notes for the disappointing report he would have to produce at some point later in the day, then slowly got up and rose to his feet. Turning to the professor one last time, he looking down at him with genuine sorrow and pity.

'Nobody can help you unless you talk to them, Avery. Just think about that.'

With a deep, heart-felt sigh, he finally walked away from the cloaked figure on the ground, making his way back over towards the cell door. With all hopes of solving the mystery dwindled away to nothing, he raised his hand up to give the steel door a couple of knocks. The knocks never came, however, because just as he was raising his hand, curling it up into a fist, the most pained voice he'd ever heard in his life rose up from somewhere behind him.

'He... He was still alive when I found him.'

It was so unexpected that for a few seconds he thought he must've been hearing things. Slowly and methodically, he turned back around, staring wide-eyed at the lonesome figure on the floor.

'What?' he whispered. 'What did you say?'

There was definitely movement down there now, a thin trembling inside the hospital gowns, just strong enough to make out through the murky dinge.

'He... He was... He was still alive.'

The voice went straight through Griffin, straight through to his core. Everything about its pitch and tone was laced with hurt, loaded and oozing with pain. Retracing his steps, he walked back along the middle of the cell, back to where he was previously sitting.

'Who was still alive? Who are you talking about?' he asked, planting himself back down on the dusty ground.

Two dark sockets stared out at him from the depths of the hood, two smudges as black as coal, but something had shifted in them now; some spark of life had been ignited.

'You... You want to know what happened?'

'Yes! Yes, I do! Tell me, Professor.'

'No. No, you don't. Y... You—'

'I want to know what happened, Professor, and I want to help you. So tell me.'

A considerable amount of time passed before the professor spoke again. Shakes and tremors were still visible under the gowns, and the faint outline of his delicate jaw jutted up and down as though he was searching for some lost reservoir of strength that might've existed within him. He must've found some somewhere, because the words eventually came; they were strained and agonising to listen to, but they came.

'I... I was in a village one day during my expedition, out in Central America. It was a tiny little place, no more than a few dozen huts...'

It felt so strange for Griffin to sit there and hear Professor Avery speak. His voice sounded just as withered and hollow as his body looked, inhuman, almost. He remained as silent as a mouse as he listened to it, however, not wanting to disrupt the flow.

'The heat...it was so intense that day, and we'd been out in it for hours. We had a guide, my...my team and I. He was an indigenous man local to the area, and he...he'd arranged a place for us to stay. We were all sweating and...and dehydrated, so none of us protested when we got to the village in the afternoon with a view to settling down early for the day. We all had notes to write up anyway, so we saw it as an opportunity to catch up with some work and recuperate.'

There was a lengthy pause from the professor. His pale, gaunt visage was hung down towards the cell floor in deep contemplation. Griffin was still completely silent, making only rough notes here and there.

'It was a beautiful place, in its...in its own way. These huts sat along the edge of a warm river, wild palm trees and long grass as far as the eye could see. The natives were so hos...hospitable...so...so welcoming.'

The mention of the native's hospitality caused the professor's voice to dip and falter even more, and Griffin sensed a touch of shame in there as well.

'Th... They cooked food for us, prepared a big meal. It... It should've been a delightful evening, but...but there was something bothering the villagers, some kind of bad atmosphere in the air. We all noticed it, and I...I eventually ended up asking the guide what was wrong. We were starting to get paranoid. We... We began to wonder whether it was something we'd done.'

It was hard for Griffin to tell whether the professor was actually looking at him or not, or whether he'd even looked at him at all since he'd entered the room. The hood sat over his head like a baggy fly net, continually reducing his features down to a vague blur.

Realising that he'd fallen silent again, Griffin gently coaxed him on.

'And what was it? What was wrong?'

'It turned out that...that the problem wasn't anything to do with us, exactly. A child h...had gone missing from the village, and they were worrying over him. He'd disappeared the evening before, and...'

'And what?' whispered Griffin, as the professor drifted off into yet another bout of silence.

'...and...nobody had seen him since.'

'And then what? What happened next?'

'After dinner we...we all retired for the night. It was still early, probably about seven o' clock, and it was still light, but we all went back to our little shacks that they'd...that they'd kindly prepared for us. It felt so good to lie down. I...I didn't have much of a bed in there, but to me, at...at that moment, it was like a luxury hotel. My legs were aching from days of trekking through the jungle, j...just resting there on the thin bed was bliss. I eventually began sorting out some notes I'd made over the previous few days. I was just lying there, putting everything in order.'

'Notes about the parasite, you mean?'

'Yes. That... That thing.'

The professor's twig-like fingers clutched at his knees at the mention of the parasite, as though he was speaking about something that went beyond evil.

'And then what?'

'I was busy organising my notes, and then...then this...this noise drifted in from outside. At first I thought it was an animal, a...a bird, maybe. It was like a...a high-pitched wailing coming from somewhere out in the trees, a whining sound in the distance that drifted in through the open window of my hut. I seemed to be the only one who could hear it. I... I eventually got up and had a look outside, and...and there was nothing there, nobody else around. B...But still, this horrible noise went on and on, and I... I just had to find out what it was. It seemed to be coming from...from the river, so I headed in that direction, following my ear. The evening was just beginning to close in by this point, and the sky was shifting into a deep, deep amber. I still had plenty of light, but...but I also knew that I had to move briskly, nonetheless. After pushing through the long grass for a while, I could see the river appearing up ahead of me, the gentle waves reflecting through the foliage. The... The screaming had also grown more acute, and...and I could tell by this point that it was coming from somewhere up in the trees. F... Following this sickly noise, I...I ended up at the base of a dead tree by the river embankment, a flaking old thing with not a single leaf on it. The faint squeals were...were coming from somewhere up in this tree, and now that I was close, I could... I could tell that they were...'

'They were what?'

'They were...human.'

Griffin's handwriting was becoming messy as he continued to jot down his notes, his fingers shaky and out of his control. 'What happened next?' he said after scrawling down the last word.

'T... There was a shape in the tree up above me. A... A round silhouette set against the amber sky. I stared at it for some time, knowing deep down what it was but...but not wanting to believe it. It was a child! No more than...than six or seven years old! He was up there in this tree...c...clinging on to one of the dead branches about thirty feet up, wailing and...wailing. His pudgy little arms and legs were wrapped around this branch and it was...it was dangling over the river! I... I have no idea how he managed to get up there, but...but there he was, as naked as the day he was born, screaming and yelling up into the dimming sky. I thought about calling for help, but...but I couldn't risk startling him and making him fall. Instead I... I silently began climbing up the tree myself, grabbing on to the flakes of dry bark and hauling myself up. It took me five minutes or so to get up there, but...but I did, and...'

'And what did you see?' Griffin whispered, watching the blurred, shadowy recesses of the professor's countenance as he re-lived his story.

'And...it was the strangest thing. T... There was no movement coming from him at all. The screams continued to come, th...they came in abundance, but...but his body was stiff and rigid. He was as still as a statue up there! Like a screaming statue! And... And there were flies on him! Dozens and dozens of flies! They were buzzing and crawling all over his little body! Buzzing all over him as he...as he clung onto this flaking branch!'

The professor was moving now, moving more than he had done so since Griffin had entered the cell. His thin arms were wrapped around his knees, hugging them tightly, and he began to rock backwards and forwards in erratic jolts, like a trauma victim pulled away from the scene of a fresh accident. His gasps and sobs shook the stiff folds of the spit hood, giving it the appearance of a deflated balloon caught in the wind.

'I... I had to get closer to him. I had to do something! Up until this point I...I'd only seen him from behind. I was looking up at him from some lower branches, look...looking up towards the back of his neck and head. The... The branches were getting thinner the further up I climbed, but...but I had to get up there. I... I almost fell into the river at one point, standing on a dry branch that snapped as soon as I put my foot on it, but...but I carried on. Wh... When I finally got up to his level I was... I was clinging on for dear life! The river glistened and splashed underneath me. It was... It was so far down.'

'What had happened to the boy, Professor?'

The hood bobbed and shook in time with the professor's tremors; he was hugging himself tighter and tighter, rocking further and further. With a strained voice, he continued.

'It was like... It was like an invisible force was holding him in place up there, gluing his body in this rigid fashion. He... He was screaming but he wasn't moving. Not even his face. And... And it was then that I saw them! H... His eyes! Oh, god, his eyes! They were open wide, looking up towards the distant clouds overhead, but...but they were... '

'They were what?'

'They... They were hideous! Big, red, and bulbous! His face and eyes were... It was a scene from a nightmare! W... Worse than anything anyone could imagine! I... I was close at this point, high up in the tree, and...and I could see it all. S... Something was going on under the surface of his eyes. S... Something was writhing and...and wr...wriggling!'

'Wriggling?'

'Eggs! Eggs and larvae! They were crawling around in his eyes! H... Hundreds of them! Th... They were moving around in there! Swimming and...and moving around!'

Griffin suddenly felt nauseous. A sickness rose up in his gut, a sickness so intense that he had to put down his notepad and pen so that he could lay a hand over his stomach.

'You're not honestly saying that the parasite...'

'The parasite was in him! It'd infected him! I... I still have no idea how it could've happened. M... Maybe he drank some infected water somewhere, or...or ate some bird droppings from the ground, I don't know, but...but the point is that somehow that *thing* managed to get inside him so that it could use him as a vehicle. It swelled his eyes and made them bulbous, turning his once-white sclera bright red. As red as...as red as...berries.'

Griffin was silent. He felt giddy, and the room seemed to tilt and turn around him.

'But... But the worst part of it all was...was that there was still life in those young eyes! There was still a person looking out of them! And... And as I hung there, holding onto the thin branches of that dead tree, he suddenly... He suddenly turned those red eyes towards me! He was looking at me! Oh, god, he was looking at me with those eyes! He... He could see me there next to him, but...but he couldn't move from his branch. His stubby arms and legs were glued in place, stiff as boards... He was... He was trapped inside his little body. That moment when... That moment when I caught his gaze...when our eyes met, it was just... His pupils were like...were like tiny black islands in seas of red larvae...moving, bubbling, writhing red seas. He was... He was fully conscious in there, looking out at me through this hive of eggs! I kept telling myself that it couldn't be true, couldn't be real, but...but there it was! Right in front of me! And... And then...'

Avery slipped into another bout of silence, another pause, but Griffin couldn't bring himself to urge him on any further, as his own voice was now reduced to a mere croak. He could do little more than wait and watch the professor, unconsciously bringing his own knees up to his chest as if mirroring his pose.

'...then there was a flash of movement, a...a flurry of wings and feathers.'

'Oh, no,' mumbled Griffin, only to himself.

'When... When that bird came down and plucked at him, he was looking right at me! That eye was looking at me as it was pecked open, the beak sinking straight into the soft jelly, sending eggs dribbling down his cheek. It... It was...'

There was some kind of eruption within the professor's hood, some kind of gurgling explosion. Suddenly, in less than a second, the thin mesh was sprayed from the inside with a rush of vomit, the hot liquid collecting into a pool as the professor hung his head over his knees. Two scrawny hands reached up and took hold of the dripping fabric, clutching it like talons. With a quick sharp tug, a reflex action, the professor ripped the wet hood from over his bony head, bile dangling from its folds. His sunken features were now completely visible and exposed, the yellow light of the overhead bulb illuminating his scalp and chiselled temples.

By the time Griffin realised he was looking into the professor's uncovered eyes, it was too late. When the hood came off, he'd been unable to look away, unable to divert his gaze. Like a motorist driving past the scene of a nasty accident and turning his head to take a look, he'd feasted his eyes on the spectacle before him, gorging greedily on its horrors. With the veil gone, the professor's face emanated something that could be felt but not described, an icy coldness that put an invisible hook in you. Up until this point, the horrid description of what the professor had seen in the tropics had been confined to the medium of words, limiting the extent to which Griffin could visualise it and understand it, but now, with that face, that expression, right there in front of him in the cell, he could somehow *see* what the professor had been describing, as though the very image itself was carved into the contours of his skin.

He felt himself slipping, falling, descending down into a hole. He was sinking down under an incredible weight, the weight of the image that'd just been transferred to him, the image that no human should be forced to endure, and he had to fight against it to keep himself above ground. Fists thrashing and lashing at the air, he struck out at this evil presence consuming him, fighting back against the horrific vision that was pushing him down. At first his hands and feet made no contact with anything, his punches and kicks stabbing at empty space, but then his blows began to land on targets, his knuckles striking the tall forms that'd gathered around him in a circle. Lashing out with frenzied fervour, he pounded away at these big white apparitions, attacking with all his might. With this vivid picture glowing and shining in front of him, haunting him with its detail, he was fighting for his life to get away from it, fighting for his very sanity, putting all of his strength into every punch and blow.

But then a tiny stabbing sensation put an end to his struggle, a single pinprick to his neck that penetrated the softness of his skin. He wasn't sinking anymore, now he was being lifted up, lifted up higher and higher by these mysterious towering white forms, their strong arms carrying his limp body away from the dust and grime of the cell floor.

The room was dim, silent, and grey. Griffin didn't know where he was, but he couldn't afford to try and work it out, either. There was a dull ache stretching across his body, throbbing away in his back, but this too could be granted no attention. Neither could the fact that his old clothes were gone, replaced with a thin baggy gown that covered his trembling body like a crumpled tent. There was only one thing that he could concentrate on now, one solitary thing that he could afford to exert his energy into: pushing the image out of his mind. It wanted dearly to enter his psyche, to penetrate the walls of his cranium, and its determination was relentless. Every ounce of his strength, every fibre of his being, went into the task of keeping this horrific picture away and diverting his attention away from it for as long as possible.

He'd been like this for hours now, pushing it away, forcing it back, trying his best to look away from it. He was like a cornered mouse in his own mind, trapped, trying desperately to fend off the menacing claws of a hungry cat. He felt as though he was fighting a losing battle, but his survival instinct wouldn't let him give up. *But how long can I actually keep this up for?* he wondered as he sat on the floor of this strange new room, his head aching from the constant strain. And he had *seen* it after all, hadn't he? He'd seen the image projected from the professor's eyes, seen its potent content, so wasn't it already lodged deep in his brain? Wasn't it already too firmly embedded in his synapses to erase? Surely it was; surely he was now stuck with it for the rest of his days, stuck with it shouting for his attention night and day with its sadistic intent?

Yes, Griffin concluded. How could he possibly keep this up? The image, the picture, wanted him too much; its desire and hunger was simply too great. With a torturous cry, reaching his personal limit, Griffin finally cracked and buckled under the immense mental pressure bearing down upon him, letting the sickly, haunting image invade his senses and consume him, swallowing him whole. And just like that, as he gave in to it, as he gave up the fight, all of the tension and struggling vanished. Leaning back against the hard concrete wall, the wall of this room he found himself in, his body slumped and his face sagged at the edges. Now that he'd succumbed to the image, letting himself get eaten and swallowed by it, all of his energy and life force drained away into nothingness. His past life, everything that he had ever wanted, everything that he formerly yearned for or lusted after, suddenly seemed pointless and trivial, nothing more than childish dreams. The image now hung like a curtain across his vision, a permanent backdrop against all that he saw, reducing everything else to monotony. The echoey sounds from out in the corridor sank away into tiny whispers, the stale smell of the room lost its edge, and the pain running down his back grew less acute. And then, once everything outside of the image was reduced to a mere sliver in his peripheral vision, a mere speck in his awareness, his eyes glazed over and his head craned down towards the floor in defeat.

MORE CHILLS FROM VELOX BOOKS

MORE CHILLS FROM VELOX BOOKS

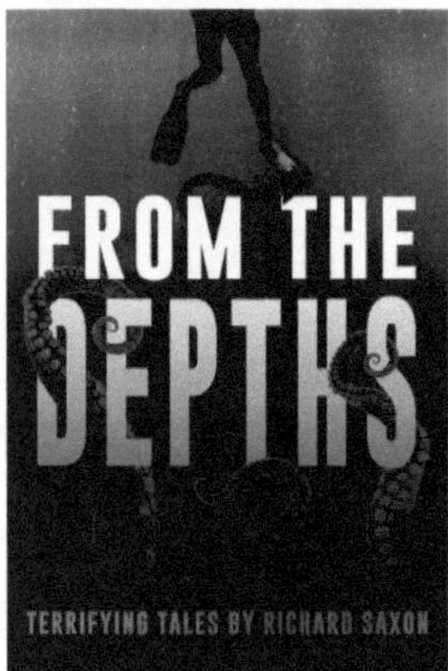

MORE CHILLS FROM VELOX BOOKS